A HEART FINDS LOVE

They galloped along so fast that it was impossible to speak even though the Duke was beside her.

Later the moon faded and the stars went out one by one. Then the first light of the rising sun appeared behind them in the East.

Of course they were riding much faster and nonstop than they had in the Prince's carriage from Batum and it was not more than an hour or so later that they saw the Port just ahead of them.

'We have done it!' Alnina wanted to cry.

But it was just impossible to speak and difficult to breathe considering the pace they had been galloping.

At the same time because the Duke was saved, she wanted to cry out with joy, but she could only say a prayer in her heart.

'Thank you, God. Thank you.'

She had saved him.

Even as she thought about it, she knew then that she loved him.

THE BARBARA CARTLAND PINK COLLECTION

Titles in this series

A HEART FINDS LOVE

BARBARA CARTLAND

Barbaracartland.com Ltd

THE BARBARA CARTLAND PINK COLLECTION

Dame Barbara Cartland is still regarded as the most prolific bestselling author in the history of the world.

In her lifetime she was frequently in the Guinness Book of Records for writing more books than any other living author.

Her most amazing literary feat was to double her output from 10 books a year to over 20 books a year when she was 77 to meet the huge demand.

She went on writing continuously at this rate for 20 years and wrote her very last book at the age of 97, thus completing an incredible 400 books between the ages of 77 and 97.

Her publishers finally could not keep up with this phenomenal output, so at her death in 2000 she left behind an amazing 160 unpublished manuscripts, something that no other author has ever achieved.

Barbara's son, Ian McCorquodale, together with his daughter Iona, felt that it was their sacred duty to publish all these titles for Barbara's millions of admirers all over the world who so love her wonderful romances.

So in 2004 they started publishing the 160 brand new Barbara Cartlands as *The Barbara Cartland Pink Collection*, as Barbara's favourite colour was always pink – and yet more pink!

The Barbara Cartland Pink Collection is published monthly exclusively by Barbaracartland.com and the books are numbered in sequence from 1 to 160.

Enjoy receiving a brand new Barbara Cartland book each month by taking out an annual subscription to the Pink Collection, or purchase the books individually.

The Pink Collection is available from the Barbara Cartland website www.barbaracartland.com via mail order and through all good bookshops.

In addition Ian and Iona are proud to announce that The Barbara Cartland Pink Collection is now available in ebook format as from Valentine's Day 2011.

For more information, please contact us at:

Barbaracartland.com Ltd.
Camfield Place
Hatfield
Hertfordshire AL9 6JE
United Kingdom

Telephone: +44 (0)1707 642629
Fax: +44 (0)1707 663041
Email: info@barbaracartland.com

THE LATE DAME BARBARA CARTLAND

Barbara Cartland who sadly died in May 2000 at the age of nearly 99 was the world's most famous romantic novelist who wrote 723 books in her lifetime with worldwide sales of over 1 billion copies and her books were translated into 36 different languages.

As well as romantic novels, she wrote historical biographies, 6 autobiographies, theatrical plays, books of advice on life, love, vitamins and cookery. She also found time to be a political speaker and television and radio personality.

She wrote her first book at the age of 21 and this was called *Jigsaw*. It became an immediate bestseller and sold 100,000 copies in hardback and was translated into 6 different languages. She wrote continuously throughout her life, writing bestsellers for an astonishing 76 years. Her books have always been immensely popular in the United States, where in 1976 her current books were at numbers 1 & 2 in the B. Dalton bestsellers list, a feat never achieved before or since by any author.

Barbara Cartland became a legend in her own lifetime and will be best remembered for her wonderful romantic novels, so loved by her millions of readers throughout the world.

Her books will always be treasured for their moral message, her pure and innocent heroines, her good looking and dashing heroes and above all her belief that the power of love is more important than anything else in everyone's life.

"I have always said that nothing is more important in the Universe than love and love lasts for ever. Real true love lasts even longer."

Barbara Cartland

CHAPTER ONE
1880

Alnina looked round the room trying to see if there was anything else she could sell.

She had already sold everything of value that she could find in the house, but there were still a large number of debts outstanding.

Her brother, Charles, had been bankrupt, although no one had been aware of it when he died.

Now she was left to save what she could of a home that had been her father's delight and joy and his father's and grandfather's before him.

Lord Lester had been, when he was a young man, very keen on travelling and as a result there were a great number of treasures in the house that he had brought from different parts of the world.

Alnina found that these had sold well and fetched much more than she anticipated.

Charles, the last of the Lester male line, as far as she knew, had been a wild spender ever since he came into the title and, because he was so handsome, he was a great success socially.

But what he really enjoyed was going off to Paris and spending a lot of money on the attractive women who had become famous all over Europe.

Alnina had at that time been at school and therefore was not aware of what her brother was doing.

Their father had always encouraged his children to learn languages and to be Cosmopolitan as well as English.

So she had stayed on an extra year at her school in Holland when she should have left, because she was very keen on learning more languages than she already knew.

Alnina had had a terrible shock when she arrived back in England.

She had learnt that her brother had fought a duel in Paris in which he was badly wounded and had died three days later.

As she had been away from home for so long, she had no idea where their other relations were or even if they had any nor did she want to seek them out and ask them to help her.

Instead she sent for her brother's Solicitor and then, to her horror, she learnt of the enormous amount of debts he had run up in the last five years since he had become Lord Lester.

"I will have to sell everything I can to meet these debts," she said to Mr. Burns the Solicitor.

"I am afraid, Miss Alnina," he then replied, "that your brother's creditors did not want to wait and were on the point, before his Lordship went abroad, of bringing a Court case against him."

"I hope they will not do that to me," Alnina asked.

"I can prevent them doing so," Mr. Burns said, "but only if you can pay them back bit by bit all that is owed."

"I will certainly do my best," she answered, "but, as you know, a large house without many acres attached to it is not particularly interesting. We are unfortunately fairly near to London and I think people who are really social want either to be in London or much farther out in the country."

Mr. Burns knew that this was true, but he was well aware that there had been no offers for the house since it had been put on the market.

Because he was a kind man and had known Alnina since she was a little girl, he had shown her how to sell the very best furniture at Christie's auction rooms in London.

He had also sent quite a number of his clients down to the house to see if there was anything they wanted to buy.

'At least,' Alnina thought to herself, 'every creditor has been given some of money, but there is still a large amount outstanding, so there must be something more that I can sell.'

But all the silver had already gone, as well as her mother's jewels.

She had already sold all the pictures that were of any value. And one or two of them proved to be valuable enough to keep most of the creditors at bay.

Now, having looked around the rooms that seemed extraordinarily empty, she walked up the stairs and into her mother's bedroom.

She had felt it was almost sacrilege to sell any of her mother's clothes. She wanted to wear them herself, but they were in some ways too old-fashioned for her.

Anyway, it was most unlikely than anyone would want to buy ball dresses that were out of date.

Her day clothes she knew would go for very small sums to the village women who would find them useful, but she was determined not to empty her mother's room completely until the very last moment.

Her dearest Mama had died when she was fifteen and she had loved her dearly.

She had been extremely fond of her father and, although she wanted to love her brother, she had seen very little of him.

He was always enjoying himself either in London or on the Continent and it was terrible to think that it was his passion for Paris that had ended in his losing his life.

'I am only so glad,' she thought as she entered her mother's bedroom, 'that Mama is not alive to know that Charles died in such a horrible way.'

Now, as she looked round the room, she thought that she would have to part with the mirror on the dressing table. It was one she had loved ever since she had been tiny.

The gilt-wood was ornamented with little cupids climbing up the sides and at the very top was a carved bird with outstretched wings.

Alnina could remember counting the cupids when she was just old enough to be able to do so. Then she had asked her mother where the bird was flying to.

"Up into the sky among the stars," her mother had said. "He is a bird and that signifies what we feel when we learn something very exciting and we lift up our hearts to Heaven."

She had not understood at the time what her mother was saying, but now, as she looked at the little bird, she thought it was something she must try to do.

It was no use to sit too gloomily in the house which was being stripped of everything that was beautiful.

She realised that the gilt mirror would fetch some money as it was antique and so would the beautiful French secretaire that stood in one corner of the bedroom.

Then, as she hated to part with them, she quickly opened the wardrobe, wondering what was left inside.

The first thing she saw at the back of it, under a white linen cover, was her mother's wedding dress.

It had always been the most fascinating dress and she could remember it ever since she was very small.

Because Lord Lester had enjoyed travelling, he had bought his wife's wedding dress on a journey he had taken while they were still engaged.

It was indeed the most unusual wedding dress that Alnina had ever seen. She had forgotten about it until now, but was sure that it would sell for a large sum.

The whole dress was decorated with the wonderful embroidery that only the Chinese could do so well and it was always believed to have been done by small boys who should really have been at school.

But to make it really spectacular, Lord Lester had ordered diamante and pink stones to add to the embroidery.

This gave it the appearance of bunches of flowers, while the bodice glittered, Alnina had always thought, as if worn by a fairy.

She took it out of the cupboard and removed the white covering and then she hung it up so that she could look at it carefully.

It must have taken years to complete and was in a perfect condition as it had only been worn once.

'I will certainly sell it,' she now thought, 'and ask a sum that should substantially reduce my debts to Charles's creditors.'

She could imagine some woman being delighted to wear it at her wedding or it would certainly enhance any museum or even perhaps be worn on the stage.

After looking at it for some time, Alnina sat down at the secretaire.

She wrote a description of the gown to be put in an advertisement and she felt certain that the way she had worded it would attract someone who was interested in anything unusual.

She was sure that there was no other wedding dress in England that could compete with this one.

'It must have cost Papa a fortune,' she mused.

He, in a way, was very much like Charles and, if he wanted something, he bought it regardless of whether he could afford it or not.

She could not help wishing that they had both been a little more sensible, as now she had to spend her time selling everything she had loved ever since she was small.

When she had finished writing the advertisement, she went downstairs.

She then found Brooks, the butler, as she still called him, who with his wife had come to the house many years before her father's death and then there had been a great number of servants.

Brooks had looked after Charles and with no other help unless he was giving a party.

It was typical of her brother, Alnina thought, when he had come home from White's Club, having lost money at the card tables, immediately to throw a large party, but she thought the noise and laughter made him forget that he was a loser.

Now Alnina was worrying, if she sold the house, what she would do with Brooks and his wife, as they were both growing older.

It would be, she knew, very difficult for them to find another place after being here for so many years.

She smiled at Brooks, whose hair – what remained of it – was white, and handed him the letter.

He would give it to the postman, if he called later in the day. It was too far for the old man to go to the village.

As the Brookses were so well known, any food Mrs. Brooks wanted was usually sent up from the shops to The Hermitage as the house was called.

"What be you selling now, Miss Alnina?" Brooks asked when she handed him the letter.

"Mama's wedding dress," Alnina answered. "I hate to let it go, but it should, because it is so unusual, fetch quite a good sum of money."

"Money! Money!" he muttered almost beneath his breath. "It's all we has to think of nowadays."

"I know and you and Mrs. Brooks have been very kind to me. So you can be sure that I will find somewhere for you in the future."

"It ain't right that you has to do all this for Master Charles," Brooks said. "He always were a naughty boy even when he was very little. He never listened to anyone, not even your father when he was alive."

There was nothing Alnina could say that she had not said already, so she therefore merely smiled at Brooks and said,

"We will win through in the end, you know that we will. You and Mrs. Brooks have been wonderful and I am very very grateful to you."

"It ain't right, Miss Alnina, when you should be going to dances and meeting young gentlemen, that you be stuck here a-worrying over money day in and day out,"

"I can think about dancing later when I have paid our debts," Alnina replied. "Mind you don't forget that letter. I just know that it will create an interest amongst the Curators of museums if no one else."

She thought a little wistfully, as she turned away, that her mother's tiara had been almost the first thing she had sold, as well as the diamond necklace that she wore at balls and the pearls she wore every day.

They had all gone very quickly and yet what she received for them was only a drop in the ocean of Charles's debts.

Now, as she went upstairs again she was wondering if she would ever get married.

And if she did, what sort of gown she would wear. It certainly would not resemble her mother's.

She had been told that it had been a sensation at the time, but several older members of the family had thought that it was too fantastic and had disapproved.

'Mama must have looked so beautiful in it,' Alnina had often said to herself.

She thought now as she walked past the mirror, which had not yet been sold, that she too would look very pretty at her wedding.

'If anyone wants to marry me and I have to pay for my own dress, it will have to be a very cheap one,' she told herself.

Then, because it was too frivolous a thought when she had to concentrate on the house, she went into another room to see what else could be sold.

It had never appealed to her to have a sale at the house and so she had only sold items one by one.

She thought on the whole it had brought in more money that if she had put them one after another under the hammer at an auction house.

At the same time it meant that raising money was much slower than a large sale would have achieved and yet she somehow could not bear to fill the house with strangers looking for a bargain.

The Hermitage was a particularly beautiful house.

It was first built in Elizabethan times and added to by various families until it fell into her great-grandfather's hands and he had improved it out of all recognition.

He made the garden beautiful and greatly admired by everyone in the County and it was still lovely but wild.

Charles had dispensed with all the gardeners except for one who was too old to be moved and now the lawns were overgrown and the weeds thick in the flowerbeds.

Yet it was still, in Alnina's eyes, the enchanted haven she had found it when she was a child.

Then the fountains had all been playing and, as she had watched them throwing their water up into the sky, she thought nothing could be more etherial.

Now every room was gradually being emptied.

As she went towards the front door, she missed the grandfather clock. It had always stood just inside the hall, but she had sold it for fifty pounds last week.

It was a clock that had delighted her as a child and when it was working there was a man at the top of it bringing down a hammer every time it struck the hour.

She had found it so fascinating when she was very small and she wondered if other children somewhere else in the country were finding it as fascinating now.

Then she told herself that it was no use thinking of the past all the time.

She had to concentrate on the future.

The most immediate problem being what would she do and where would she go if the house was sold.

She was hoping that whoever bought it would take on the Brookses, but she herself would have to leave.

'Where can I go and what can I do?' she asked and could find no answer.

Then, as she walked across the lawn, she looked up at the sky and saw a bird flying high overhead.

'Perhaps,' she now told herself, 'he will carry my thoughts into an enchanted land where everything I want will come true.'

Then she laughed at herself.

It was the sort of thought she had had when she was growing up and then the world seemed an intriguing place waiting for her to explore it.

Because her father always talked of his travels, she wanted to travel too.

She imagined herself visiting different places in the world which so far she had only read about in books and it was this yearning for something so different, something so exciting, that had made her concentrate on languages when she was at school.

She had read all the books she could find on each country whose language she had been taught to speak.

There were French books that she read avidly once she knew French. There were German books, which she did not find so delightful as she thought that German was an ugly language.

But she had loved Italian, Greek and Spanish.

Then, just when she was nearly eighteen and should have been leaving to have a Season in London, she found herself captivated by Russian.

As Russian history books were so interesting, they helped her to overcome the difficulties of the language.

'Now,' she thought as she looked up at the sky, 'I will never see the places I have read about and which Papa always found entrancing.'

The one thing she was absolutely sure of was that she could not now afford to travel, unless, of course, she could become a teacher to the children of Diplomats.

Or she could become a secretary at an Embassy, otherwise she would have to be content with books instead of reality.

It was sad, but, because she did not want to feel unhappy about herself, she walked back into the house.

She was thinking that there were still parts of it she had not fully explored where there might still be something saleable.

Her advertisement appeared in *The Times* four days later.

Brooks brought the newspaper in with breakfast and he had opened it so that she could read at a glance what she had written.

'If that does not attract people,' she thought to herself, 'then nothing will.'

She hoped that she would obtain the one thousand pounds she was asking for and not have to reduce it.

She had learnt that many people, who were buying anything, always expected to get it for less than the seller asked.

So after the first two or three items she had sold, she always asked a price a little higher than she expected to receive.

She had, in fact, at the very last moment, increased the price she was asking for the wedding dress and so she would be prepared to reduce it, but, of course, appear reluctant as she did so.

"Well, I expects," Brooks was saying, "you'll have them knocking on the door to have a look at it. But if you asks me, you could have asked for even more than that."

"I don't think anyone spends more on a wedding dress," Alnina replied. "In fact, I have seen advertisements offering them with a veil and a wreath for half that price."

"Yes, but what they be selling ain't a dress like your Mama's," Brooks insisted. "Your father always said it were the prettiest gown in the whole world."

Alnina laughed.

"That is the sort of thing Papa would say. But one thousand pounds is a great deal of money these days and most brides have to buy their whole trousseau for less."

"There be brides and brides," Brooks said. "If you asks me, Miss Alnina, you could have got more than that."

"I have not received anything yet," Alnina replied. "But we will soon find out if you are right, Brooks, and I am wrong."

Brooks did not reply.

But she heard him mutter to himself as he carried her empty tray out of the dining room towards the kitchen.

*

She would have been most interested if she had known that at the very moment when she was arguing with Brooks about her advertisement, the Duke of Burlingford was reading *The Times* in his London house.

It had been put neatly down on his breakfast table on a silver stand, which had been used by his grandfather.

He glanced at the headlines, but then he was really thinking how extraordinary it was that he should be seated in a beautiful carved chair at the head of the table.

He was now ensconced in a house that he had only visited three or four times before it became his.

In fact, he still felt as if he was in a dream from which he would not wake up.

He found it quite impossible to believe that he was now actually the Head of the Family and he had never in his wildest dreams thought it would be possible.

John Ford, as he had been born, had at an early age wanted to travel.

When he left Eton, where he had a good education, he had rejected his father's advice that he should go on to a University.

Instead he had set off to explore the world and he had found it so much more fascinating and educational than any University could have been.

He had travelled for four years and then he returned home because he learnt that his father was ill.

His father owned a nice comfortable, medium-sized house in Worcestershire and he was not very interested in anything that took place outside his own County.

He was, however, an ardent enthusiast for sporting activities. He rode to hounds, had a small but excellent shoot of his own and was a patron of a local cricket team and this he had founded and financed.

He had only one son with his wife, who was not particularly strong.

When she died, he was quite content to live on his own with only periodical news of his son.

He saw very little of the Head of the Family, who was the Duke of Burlingford, the owner of an enormous estate in Sutherland in Scotland as well as a family house in Berkeley Square.

Once a year the Duke expected his relations to visit him in the huge house which had been given to the first Duke by Charles II for his loyalty and support.

When John Ford met his relatives there, the Duke entertained them lavishly and they would go home thinking what a charming man he was.

It was obvious that his care for the family would be continued by his son who was very like him.

His son, however, seemed to have no wish to marry and the older members of the family pressed him to choose a charming wife. But at thirty-one he was still a bachelor despite their protests.

John Ford, however, was not particularly interested in the Dukedom or his cousin, who was five years older than he was.

"You go, Papa," he would say when a summons to a family get-together arrived.

It was an order that few of his relations were brave enough to refuse.

"You should take more of an interest in the family," his father would reply.

"I know, Papa, but you know how boring it is with all those old relations and the Duke lecturing us at almost every meal."

His father had laughed.

"I will tell him you are in Timbuktu. I did that last year and he accepted it. But I cannot help thinking as I am getting old that just as he keeps telling your cousin that he should marry, I should be saying the same to you."

John had, however, refused.

Then, when he was in South America, his father had died unexpectedly during an extremely cold winter.

He thought perhaps that his father had been right and he should find a wife.

As it happened, he fell in love quite unexpectedly with a young girl who was the beauty of the Season.

One of his relatives had invited him to stay for a ball she was giving for her daughter, Marcia, who had just come out and John, who was twenty-three, had accepted because he could not think of a good enough excuse for refusing.

He had gone to the ball, thinking that he would enjoy himself far more if he went to his Club and played bridge.

Marcia was only eighteen, exceedingly pretty and undoubtedly one of the sensations of the Season.

They had danced together and when John, a little later, asked her to marry him, she accepted.

He was in a seventh Heaven of delight and indeed so apparently was his future wife.

The wedding was announced and planned to take place in a month's time.

John was very busy redecorating his home and he wanted it to be a fitting background for the beauty of his future wife. His father had left it exactly as it was when he inherited and there was therefore a great deal to do to make it what John considered perfect for Marcia.

She liked pink, so the bedroom was decorated for her in that colour and he bought new curtains and re-gilded the carved and gilt-canopied bed, which had been there since his ancestor had been given it by Charles II.

It was not a large house and did not in any way compare with the Ducal residence, which was very big and very imposing.

"We will be very happy," John had told his pretty fiancée, "and there are so many places I want to show you in the world. So we will travel as much as we can."

Marcia agreed to everything.

The wedding was finally fixed for the second week in May and it was then that John had a letter from the Duke telling him that he was unable to be present at the wedding.

However, he would be giving John, as a member of the family, a picture of one of their ancestors and also a canteen of silver engraved with the family crest.

John thanked him politely and then hurried back to Marcia, only to find what he had never expected in his wildest imagination.

Waiting for him at his home was a letter and, when he opened it eagerly, it was to read that Marcia would not be marrying him as had been planned.

She had fallen in love with a young man who was a Viscount and would, when his father died, become an Earl.

To John it was a blow he had never anticipated.

He realised cynically and with a bitterness he did not attempt to hide, that Marcia had only become engaged to him because he was related to the Duke.

There was no thought of his inheriting the title, so she had eagerly accepted the Viscount instead.

Rather than face the sympathy of his friends, John had left England immediately and gone abroad.

This time he went to Russia and spent some time in the Caucasus and when he finally returned home, he was three years older and very cynical about women.

"I have made a fool of myself once," he told his friend William Armstrong, who had accompanied him on several of his trips, "but once bitten, twice shy and now I will never marry."

It was easy to say that when he was just John Ford and of no particular consequence.

Now it was very different.

By what had seemed an impossibility, he became the Duke of Burlingford.

The Duke and his son and heir had decided that they would go to Scotland in August to shoot grouse and to fish for salmon.

In the previous year they had found it a long and tedious journey overland, so they had decided that this year they would go by sea.

The Duke's Scottish castle and estate lay a long way to the North and to travel by sea seemed a far more comfortable and more sensible way of getting there.

Then there blew up, however, an unexpected and unusually violent storm in the North Sea and they had very nearly reached their destination when the ship they were travelling in was driven onto a rocky shore.

There was no chance of saving anyone on board and both the Duke and his son were drowned.

John Ford was informed with difficulty, because he was in Nepal at the time, that he was now the tenth Duke of Burlingford.

To say that he was pleased was not entirely true.

He was surprised, in fact astonished, and thought it would undoubtedly be rather a bore to become Head of a Family that he had paid very little attention to in the past.

Then when his friend, William Armstrong, arrived to see him, almost the first thing he said was,

"You will hardly believe me, William, but what I am thinking now is that we can buy that mountain in the Caucasus."

William stared at him.

"We were certain that there was gold in it, but we did not have the money to bid for it at the time."

William gasped in astonishment.

"Are you still thinking of the prospect?" he asked.

"Indeed I am. You must remember how much we enjoyed that trip through Georgia and on to the Caucasus."

William nodded and the Duke went on,

"We were both convinced that the mountain which we climbed and inspected so carefully contained gold."

"They say that about many of the mountains in the Caucasus," William commented. "But, as it would have cost a fortune to make sure of it, we had to leave well alone."

"Of course we did then, but now I have plenty of money and there is nothing to stop us from buying that mountain."

"Now that you are talking about it, I can tell you something I discovered last year when you were not with me," William said. "I went to Georgia and actually met the owner of the mountain you were so interested in."

"You met him! You never told me."

"What was the point?" William asked. "I recalled how disappointed you were when, after we were certain we had found gold, we were told its owner had no intention of selling."

"I remember that."

"Now I was told," William went on, "that he might sell it, but wants a high price for it. I had no wish to upset you by saying that it was 'hands off' as far as we were concerned."

"Of course it was then," the Duke agreed. "But now I am a Duke, although Heaven knows I will make a very bad one, I am determined that whatever you may say or think, that particular mountain will be mine."

William lay back in his chair and laughed.

"You are always the same, John," he sighed. "You make up your mind about something and then nothing will make you change it. Who would believe for one second that, having become a Duke when you had least expected it, your only thoughts are of buying a mountain, which, if you obtain it, it may quite easily be a disappointment."

"Nevertheless it will be a satisfaction to me," John replied, "simply because I had thought it could never be mine. Therefore I will at least have achieved something in my life."

"I think you have already achieved a great deal. Very few people know the world as well as you know it and we have had a great deal of fun, even though we had to travel on the cheap."

"I want that mountain!" the Duke insisted firmly. "And now I can afford to buy it."

There was a pause and then William remarked,

"I have just told you that I met Prince Vladimir Petrov late last year. He is a tough creature and has one ambition in his life, I was told."

"What is that?" the Duke asked.

"He wants his daughter, and he has only one, to marry an English Nobleman."

"Are you making this up, William?"

"No, I am telling the truth. It did not sound all that interesting, especially as I am never likely to have a title. Therefore I merely thought that perhaps sooner or later the Prince would achieve what he wanted."

"Why on earth should he want an Englishman for his daughter?"

"I think because the Czar and Queen Victoria are at daggers drawn," William answered, "the Prince wants to be different. Also, as Britain is very powerful, if there is a war, he wants to be on the winning side."

"Well, all I can say is that I am sure, as his daughter is a Princess, that she will find some idiot who will marry her. But it will not be me."

"Don't you be too certain about that, John. These Russians, especially when they are Georgians, are not only determined when they have an aim in life, but are also extremely shrewd and even unscrupulous about it."

"What are you trying to say to me?"

"I am trying to save you from yourself," William replied. "I am quite certain, if we go back now and tell the Prince we want to buy his mountain, he will think, because you are a Duke that you are exactly what he wants for his daughter."

There was silence for a moment.

Then William said,

"Don't be stupid, John. You know as well as I do there are a dozen different ways a man can be forced to the altar even if he does not want it. Remember that Russians are extremely clever at achieving what they desire."

"I want that mountain," the Duke said stubbornly.

"At the expense of your freedom?" William asked.

"No certainly not! I have told you before and I will tell you again that, after the way I was treated, I have no intention of marrying any woman, however attractive she may be."

"Very well then," William said. "Unless you want to commit suicide or provide yourself willy-nilly with a Russian wife, you must not go to the Caucasus."

The Duke knocked his knuckles together.

"I intend to go," he asserted, "and no one, not even you, William, will be able to stop me."

William made a helpless gesture with his hands, but the Duke went on,

"There must be ways and means of insuring myself against the bonds of matrimony. In fact I will bet you a thousand pounds to a three-penny bit that I purchase the mountain without being married to the Princess, whatever she may look like."

"I will certainly take you up on that," William said. "At the same time be sensible, John. I cannot allow you to walk straight into a fiery furnace."

He paused for a moment before he continued,

"Everyone told me when I was there last year that Prince Vladimir is absolutely determined that his daughter should marry an English Nobleman. He was even writing to Queen Victoria about her."

"I don't suppose for one second that Her Majesty would even reply to that."

"No, of course not!" William agreed. "Equally what is the point of getting your fingers burnt, perhaps even being bumped off, for not doing what the Prince wants you to do?"

"You seem to think that I am a silly fool," the Duke answered, "and that is where you are mistaken."

He picked up *The Times*, which was still spread out on its silver stand.

"I was just looking at this advertisement when you arrived and wondering who it could have been made for. After all no one would know better than you and I about exquisite Chinese embroidery and this wedding dress does certainly sound unusual."

William caught the newspaper when it was thrown to him and now he was looking at it in a puzzled fashion until he saw the advertisement.

"I don't understand," he quizzed. "If you buy a wedding dress, who are you buying it for?"

"What I am going to do," the Duke said slowly, as if he was thinking it out, "is to buy the wedding dress and have a photograph taken of my wife wearing it. She will, of course, not be travelling with me."

For a moment William did not comprehend exactly what he was saying and then he sat back in his chair and roared out with laughter.

"Really, John, you never cease to surprise me and only you could think of anything so clever."

"I thought you would appreciate my little plan," the Duke said. "Now William, how soon shall we leave to go and beg, borrow or steal this outstanding wedding dress in which my mythical wife will look so attractive?"

CHAPTER TWO

Alnina looked excitedly for the post the next day.

She was somewhat disappointed to find that there was only one letter from a shop. It advertised their own wedding dresses that were at reasonable prices.

However, there was still a great deal to be done in other parts of the house.

She went from room to room picking up the pieces that she thought would sell, even though the very best had already gone.

She then went to the stables to see the last two horses she had left.

Her brother had assembled quite a good collection because, like her, he loved riding. Unfortunately he also enjoyed betting and he had lost a considerable amount of money on the Racecourses.

He had, in fact, sold the best of his horses for a good sum of money before he died, but that had vanished too.

Now there were only two horses left and Alnina was determined to keep them if she possibly could.

'I must have something to get about on.' she told herself.

She was already planning at the back of her mind that, if she sold the house, she might well keep one of the cottages on the estate for herself. In which case she would take all the furniture she needed from the house.

It was just an idea and it would only be possible if she was left with enough money to live on.

At the moment there was still a pile of unpaid bills, even though it was not as large as it had been.

'I must be absolutely clear of Charles's debts,' she muttered to herself, 'before I can even begin to think of my own comforts.'

She supposed that if the worst came to the worst she could teach languages, although it was something she had never anticipated she might have to do.

Yet sooner than starve she could at least qualify as a teacher, considering how well she spoke so many foreign languages.

At the same time she was sensible enough to know that her youth and her looks were against her. She was quite sure that she did not look her age.

Without being at all conceited, she knew that most people would not want a young and very pretty girl in their house who obviously did not belong to the schoolroom.

She remembered that her own Governesses were middle-aged cosy women and they never ate downstairs in the dining room if there was a party. They would take it for granted that, when there were guests, they would stay in the schoolroom.

'It's no use me thinking about the future,' she told herself, 'until I am clear of the past and that seems likely to take a long time.'

She then went into the kitchen garden to see if there were any vegetables for her luncheon. She found some potatoes, which were small, but if cooked well they could be delicious.

She was carrying them back for Mrs. Brooks, when, as she came round the outside of the house, she saw to her surprise that there was a very smart chaise outside the front door. It was drawn by four perfectly matched horses.

As she walked nearer, she saw that the chaise had a crest on the outside of the door and she did not know of anyone in the County who had such a smart chaise or such fine horses.

The groom, who was standing at their heads, wore a livery she did not recognise.

Hoping she looked tidy, she hurried into the house to find Brooks waiting for her in the hall.

"There be a gentleman to see you, Miss Alnina," he said, "and he says he be the Duke of Burlingford."

Alnina stared at him in surprise.

But Brooks, obviously thrilled at such an important visitor, was already walking ahead of her to open the door into the study.

Instinctively Alnina put her hand up to her hair to tidy it and then, putting down the potatoes on the nearest table, she followed Brooks towards the study.

She wondered why she had never heard of the Duke of Burlingford before.

'It could well be an elderly friend of Papa's,' she reflected, 'who has just heard of Charles's death.'

Brooks opened the door and she walked in.

A tall young man was standing looking out of the window and, when he turned round, Alnina thought that he was very handsome and certainly not likely to be a friend of her father's.

He walked towards her, holding out his hand.

"I have learnt that your name is Miss Lester," he began, "and I think I knew your brother, Charles, who was at Eton with me. He was younger than me, but I remember he was selected for the cricket team at a very early age."

Alnina smiled and then replied,

"I suppose you do not know that Charles is dead."

"Dead!" the Duke exclaimed. "But why should he have died? He was a good deal younger than me."

"He died after fighting a duel in France and you could not have seen it in the newspapers. It was reported, I think, as a warning to other young men who could get into trouble in Paris."

"I am sorry, very sorry to hear of Charles's death," the Duke said, "but I really came to see you because of your advertisement in *The Times*. It did not give your name, only the address."

"So that is why you have come here, Your Grace. I wondered, when I saw your horses outside and admired them very much, who you could possibly be."

"I have only recently come into the Dukedom," the Duke replied, "owing to a disaster that happened to my cousin and his son at sea."

"Oh, I did read about that. I was wondering where I had heard your name before and now I remember."

"Unfortunately I did not read about your brother," the Duke added. "But I am really sorry to hear the news."

"I am sorry too," Alnina said. "But sadly Charles left a great number of debts and to pay them off I am trying to sell the house and more or less everything in it."

"It is a very beautiful house, Miss Lester. In fact, as I came up the drive, I thought it was one of the most attractive houses I have seen for a long time."

"I love it because it is my home," Alnina admitted, "but it has to go, like almost everything else in it."

She glanced up as she was speaking at the empty space over the mantelpiece where a picture had hung and she had been lucky to receive three hundred pounds for it.

As if he was reading her thoughts, the Duke said,

"I know what you must be feeling."

"Now we should talk business, Your Grace. You came to see the wedding dress and it would be helpful if you would not mind coming up to the bedroom to view it."

"Of course I will do so."

The Duke thought as he spoke that Charles's sister was certainly very attractive and he recalled that Charles had been a very good-looking boy.

It seemed sad that she should have to sell the family house and its contents.

'Surely,' he thought, 'there must be a successor who would carry on the Lester family.'

Alnina, however, was walking towards the door and he followed her.

The Duke was well aware, as they walked up the stairs, that there were gaps where furniture had once stood and a great number of empty spaces on the walls. It was easy to see where the pictures had hung as the wallpaper was fresh, whilst the walls themselves were obviously in need of decorating.

Alnina, without speaking, led the Duke along the passage where the best bedrooms were situated.

She opened the door into her mother's room and the sunshine streaming in through the windows made it seem, with its elegant gilt bed and cupid-decorated mirror, very charming.

The wedding dress was hanging on the outside of the wardrobe where Alnina had left it and the rays of the sun were shimmering brightly on the diamante and making the whole gown sparkle.

The Duke stared at it and then he said,

"It is magnificent, the finest wedding dress I have ever seen."

"I thought you would think so," Alnina answered. "My father bought it in China and my mother wore it at their wedding. Otherwise it has never been used."

"I suppose really you were keeping it for yourself," the Duke enquired.

Alnina laughed and shook her head.

"I think it would now appear very peculiar in any English Church and, if indeed I did marry, I would want something less spectacular."

"Well, it's exactly what I want," the Duke said.

"I suppose you have asked your wife if she will wear anything so unusual, Your Grace?" Alnina asked.

The Duke smiled.

"Now I must explain that there is no wife, but I want, if you would like the truth, to pretend that there is one."

Alnina looked puzzled.

"I don't understand," she murmured.

"Are you really interested in selling it?"

"Of course I am. You said you liked the wedding dress and I admit that it is very beautiful. Yet, although I should not say so, since I am anxious to sell it, I think that most young women would feel rather embarrassed to wear anything so fancy at an ordinary wedding."

Then she suddenly put up both her hands as if to apologise and added quickly,

"I should not have said that! Because you are a Duke, your wedding will not be ordinary."

"As I have already told you, although you have not understood, there is no bride."

He saw the baffled expression on Alnina's pretty face and went on,

"I am pretending to be a married man because I fervently wish to buy something very special from a certain foreigner and he is determined, because he is a Prince, that his daughter will marry an English aristocrat."

Alnina laughed.

"I have heard of that happening in a number of families abroad and naturally an English Duke would make a very special and distinguished bridegroom."

"Which I have no intention of being – "

"Then why do you want a wedding dress?"

"Because I am going to pretend, as I said, that I am married, so that there will be no question of being hurried up the aisle in some obscure church – perhaps at pistol-point – to marry a girl who cannot even speak English."

Alnina laughed again.

"That certainly would be an unpleasant situation," she said, "to say the least of it."

"I will buy your wedding dress, Miss Lester, but I think I must make it a condition that you find me someone who will be photographed in it as my wife."

"Are you really serious?" Alnina questioned him. "It does seem such an extraordinary thing to do, but I can understand you not wishing to have a Prince, whoever he may be, pushing his daughter into your arms."

"I can see you are as quick-witted as your brother used to be at school," the Duke replied. "I remember he found a special way of getting someone else to do his out-of-school work when he wanted to be on the cricket field!"

"That sounds very like Charles," Alnina said. But go on telling me about this Prince you have to deceive."

"It's quite simple, I want to buy something from him that he will not part with very easily. And he has a daughter and he is completely determined that she will marry an English Nobleman."

He gave a sigh as he continued,

"It does not require a very clever brain to realise that he will only give me what I want if I give him what he wants."

"So you are going to be very clever," she replied, "and tell the Prince that you are already married."

"Exactly! Now you have the whole story. All I need now is a photograph of my bride. Then there will be no question of having to look twice at the Princess who I expect is rather plain anyway!"

Alnina chuckled, as she could not help it, thinking that it was the most extraordinary story she had ever heard.

At the same time the wedding dress, which had so delighted her father would fit in very well with his plan.

What also pleased her was the fact that the wedding dress would be sold to someone as important as the Duke and she was quite certain that sooner or later he would find a wife who would wear it, if only as fancy dress.

She was too tactful, however, to say this aloud and simply asked,

"How soon will you want the photograph? And do you really expect me to find someone to wear the gown?"

She was thinking as she spoke that there were very few girls in the village who would look attractive enough to be marrying a Duke.

There was only poor old Mrs. Brooks and herself in the house –

Then she gave a sudden exclamation.

"But, of course!" she cried. "As you are being kind enough to buy the gown from me, I can easily wear it just for the photograph."

"That is what I was hoping you would say, Miss Lester. You will look very lovely in it and no one will be surprised at my choice of a bride."

"Then, of course, I shall be only too willing to be photographed and I suppose you will be beside me."

There was silence and then the Duke said,

"I had not thought of that, but naturally, if it was your wedding, you would hardly be standing alone."

"No, of course not and I have the veil, although I have sold Mama's tiara that she wore at the wedding, but I can easily make a wreath out of real flowers.

"That sounds just what I want," the Duke replied. "I will bring a photographer down tomorrow, if that suits you and I suppose that I will have to change into my best clothes as the bridegroom."

"If you are marrying abroad," she suggested, "you will be wearing evening dress, as you know they always do in France."

"Yes, of course they do. Well, evening dress it will be and, as it is to impress, I had better put on my father's decorations. And if there are not enough of them, then my relative, the previous Duke, had a large number."

"As he was not your father, it must have been a great surprise for you to come into the title, Your Grace."

She was just following her own thoughts and, when she had spoken them aloud, she thought that perhaps it was rather impertinent.

But the Duke remarked,

"I had never dreamt at any time in my life that I might become the Duke of Burlingford. But then I am not complaining."

"I should think not!" Alnina exclaimed.

"In fact," the Duke continued, "I find life is very pleasantly different from what it has been before, when I had to count every penny before I spent it."

"You could not then have afforded an expensive wedding dress like this, Your Grace?"

"At the moment I am thinking it is cheap at the price. Can I ask you to keep it for me until I return from my visit abroad? I will then display it in my house in the country, which in parts looks like a museum."

"I have indeed heard of Burlingford Hall and how magnificent it is," Alnina said.

"Then it is certainly something that you should see when I come back from the Caucasus," the Duke said.

Alnina gave a little cry.

"Are you really going to the Caucasus?" she asked, "how fascinating! It is something I have always wanted to do myself and I think there are more stories about those strange Caucasian mountains than about anywhere else."

"They mean a lot to me," the Duke said, "and when I return, still a bachelor thanks to your wonderful wedding dress, I will tell you all about it."

"It's a promise you must keep. In the meantime I will find somewhere where we can be photographed, which will look as if a wedding is really taking place."

"That is most kind of you and then I will be here tomorrow afternoon at three o'clock. As soon as I have changed into my wedding clothes we will be photographed. Shall I pay you now or tomorrow for the gown?"

Alnina drew in her breath.

It seemed marvellous she could have made so much money with so little effort.

When the men, who had bought pieces of furniture came to the house, they had spent hours looking at them from every angle and they made sure that they were taking the best of the particular pieces they required.

One man, who had wanted to buy a writing table, had insisted on going into every room before he finally decided to buy the one he had seen first.

Alnina realised that the Duke was waiting for her to answer his question and she replied,

"I would be most grateful if I could have the one thousand pounds immediately as there are so many people waiting for their payment. When one gets paid, the others are not so pressing as they are when I have nothing to give any of them!"

"I understand. If I can sit down at your writing table, Miss Lester, I will give you a cheque."

"You will be more comfortable downstairs," Alnina suggested.

The Duke took a last look at the wedding dress.

"It is certainly the finest I have ever seen," he said, "and actually I have been to China."

"How lucky you are. I would love to go to the East and I will think of you amongst the wonderful mountains of the Caucasus. Are you going to climb them?"

"I hope so."

As the Duke spoke, he thought that it would be a mistake to tell anyone why he was going back there and what he was really seeking.

He walked to the door and Alnina followed him.

"Do you really have to sell this house?" he asked as they walked down the stairs, "and if you do, where are you going to live?"

"I wish I knew the answer to that question, but unfortunately Charles's debts have to be paid and there are still a great number outstanding."

The Duke thought it very hard on her, but after all it was not his business and, as he walked into the study, he told himself that it would be a mistake to become involved.

He wrote out a cheque for one thousand pounds and he could see by the delight in Alnina's bright eyes how much it meant to her.

In spite of his desire not to be involved he asked,

"Surely you have relatives who would help you pay off Charles's debts?"

"They are all very old and the majority of them are quite poor, Your Grace. I remember Papa was thought of as the rich man of the family, but even he could not employ as many people as he wished to on the land and we were obliged to cut down the servants in the house."

"I suppose that would happen in a great number of families," the Duke said.

He thought as he spoke it was an idiotic remark.

No families of his acquaintance had had their sons killed in a duel.

"I expect I will manage," Alnina said bravely, "and thank you, thank you for helping me with this cheque. I can assure you it will be very gratefully received by those who have waited so long to be paid."

She was speaking, he mused lightly, which showed how grave she was being.

As he walked towards the front door, he thought again that it was very sad for such a young and pretty girl to have to cope with anything so overwhelming.

He picked up his hat from the hall and now, as he walked down the steps, he was thinking again that it would be silly of him to become involved even though this pretty girl had supplied him with exactly what he required for his own problem.

As they reached the chaise, the Duke said,

"Thank you once again for saying that I may come tomorrow and be photographed with you. I forgot to tell you that I don't want anyone to see the pictures or to learn that they have even been taken."

"I understand and I promise no one will know you have come here again except the old servants who have been with us ever since I was born. They would never do anything I ask them not to do."

"It's all too good to be true," the Duke sighed, "and I will be here tomorrow at exactly three o'clock, as we have arranged – and thank you again."

"That is what I should be saying to you."

He stepped into the chaise and picked up the reins.

As the groom hurried to jump up behind him, the Duke raised his hat and Alnina waved to him.

She watched the chaise until it disappeared amongst the oak trees at the end of the drive.

Then she walked back into the house to find Brooks in the hall.

"I have sold Mama's wedding dress," she told him with obvious relief.

"That be good news, Miss Alnina. "I never thought that'd go. In fact, I says to the Missus, I says, that'll still be on our hands when everything else be gone."

"The Duke is coming again tomorrow as he wants to photograph it, but he has no wish for anyone to know he has bought it. Of course I told him that we never talk to any outsider of what happens here."

"One of the reasons, Miss Alnina, be there be no one to talk to," Brooks remarked. "I were only saying to the Missus a day or two ago that since you've been home there's been no one hardly to say a word to."

Alnina knew this to be true.

"You would think having known your father for so long," Brooks went on, "they'd have been coming to tell you how sorry they be about Master Charles."

Alnina knew that the people around them were on the whole embarrassed by the circumstances of Charles's death and they had kept away from what could have been an uncomfortable conversation.

"I am perfectly happy," she said, "to have you and Mrs. Brooks to talk to. But I expect His Grace will want a cup of tea when he calls tomorrow. So do ask your wife to make one of her delicious cakes."

"That'll please her. She's been feeling that she be wasted here with only you, Miss Alnina, to cook for."

Alnina, who had heard this before, said quickly,

"Well, tomorrow she will have a Duke and I am sure that there will be visitors as soon as they think I am more settled."

She knew that what she was really saying was that when their friends heard she was selling the furniture and pictures in the house, they might call, hoping to pick up a bargain.

She walked into the study and looked again at the Duke's cheque.

She had decided already to divide it amongst two large creditors who were being rather more impatient than the rest. If they were pleased, which they surely should be, they would not harass her as much as they had been doing.

She had made it very plain to them the last time they had called that she could not give them what she did not have.

Then she remembered that she had to find the veil which was somewhere amongst her mother's things, also to make the wreath for her head and a bouquet for her to hold.

She only hoped there were enough white flowers in the garden and the sooner she picked them the less rush there would be tomorrow morning.

A wreath, as she well knew, could be difficult to make look really attractive and it would take time, however skilfully she made it.

Anyway, she was exceedingly grateful to the Duke for providing her with one thousand pounds.

For some reason she could not really explain, she was determined that the photograph should impress and convince the Prince for whom all this trouble was being taken.

*

If Alnina was elated, so was the Duke.

He drove back triumphantly to his large house in Berkeley Square.

As he expected, William was waiting for him and exclaimed as he entered the drawing room,

"You are late, John! You told me that you would be back before this."

"I am late, but I have been very successful."

"I just don't believe it. The wedding dress sounded impossible and, in fact, I was certain it was a hoax."

"It was nothing of the sort," the Duke retorted. "It is the most fantastic piece of Chinese embroidery I have ever seen and you will think so too."

"So have you brought it back with you, John?"

"No. We will be going there tomorrow and you are going to take several photographs of me with my bride."

"Are you joking?" William asked him.

"No! I am telling you the truth," the Duke replied. "The girl who is selling the gown is the sister of Charles

Lester. Do you remember him at Eton? A very good-looking chap. He got into the cricket eleven when he was still very young."

"Of course, I remember Charles. He was my fag at one time and very tiresome he was. I do admit that I was always rather suspicious that he sneaked my money as well as my chocolates!"

"I would not be surprised. Apparently he was killed in a duel in Paris and you know those duels always take place because someone has been making a fool of himself in some way or another."

"Is that how Charles died?" William asked.

"Yes, and leaving huge debts. His sister, who is a very pretty girl, is having to raise money to pay off his creditors, which includes selling their house and everything in it."

"Good heavens!" William exclaimed. "So Charles must have been behaving worse than usual. I remember he was a reckless gambler as he grew older and I used to see him at White's playing at the tables. Now I think about it, I remember someone telling me that he had lost a large amount of money racing."

"So this wretched girl has to sell everything that they possess," the Duke said. "But she has kindly offered to be photographed with me purporting to be my wife."

He laughed before he added,

"That will certainly prevent the Prince from trying to marry me off to his daughter!"

"All I can say is that you are very clever and very lucky, John. I ask you, who else would find a wedding dress and a substitute bride in twenty-four hours?"

"It does seem so extraordinary, but everything has fallen into my hands like a ripe peach. She is a Lady and a very pretty one and she looks exactly the sort of bride a Duke should have, as those foreign fellows would expect."

"Very well," William agreed. "It should protect you against the Prince."

"Well, you just have to admit, William, that I have saved myself and now, as we can well afford it, let's have some champagne as I am thirsty after driving all that way."

"I am just thinking," William said, "that my camera is not a particularly good one, although it does produce a photograph of a sort."

The Duke stared at him.

"In which case why did you not say so before?" he asked. "Of course I will want a good photograph, but it would be a mistake, as you well know, for me to call in a professional photographer who would undoubtedly talk."

"Of course it would. The Duke of Burlingford is an important fellow and a social catch is always news!"

"All right, all right, William! You have made your point, but for Heaven's sake do go and buy yourself a first class camera and then I will give it to you as a birthday present."

"You have given me one recently," William said. "If you remember, I was twenty-two at the time."

"Well, it can be your Christmas present," the Duke said, "and you might as well have the best while you are about it."

"I most certainly will. I would like a new camera and, who knows, I might, while you are negotiating for that tedious mountain you insist on buying, take photographs of the Caucasian people who we know so very little about."

"Only because they live in the back of beyond and that, my Dear William, is why we have been lucky enough to find gold in a remote mountain, which no one else has discovered before."

"Well, the mountain was still there when I passed it last year, but Heaven knows whether or not the gold is still there. After all, it's nearly four years since we found it."

"I am quite certain that the Prince then had no idea there was gold on his land and, if he did find it later, you would have heard about it."

"You may be right or you may be wrong," William pointed out. "But I am perfectly willing to come with you. I always enjoy Georgia, it has a charm that very few other countries can boast."

"That is what I have always felt," the Duke said. "But I want to make quite certain I don't have to marry one of their women."

"You will have to marry someone sooner or later," William remarked.

"Why? I have learnt my lesson where women are concerned and I want to make it quite clear, once and for all, that I will *never* marry."

He gave a laugh before he went on,

"I was foolish enough to think that I was in love when I was comparatively young, but now I have enough common sense just to play the field."

"Well, you then bet me a thousand pounds to a threepenny bit and that one thousand pounds is what I am determined to win," William said. "It will not only be Prince Vladimir Petrov trying to get you up the aisle with his daughter, but I will be pushing from behind."

The Duke picked up a cushion and threw it at him.

"You are making a nuisance of yourself, William. I have heard quite enough of all this from my relatives and you know as well as I do that I have no intention of making a fool of myself for a second time. Once is quite enough."

William did not answer.

Then unexpectedly the Duke laughed again.

"I am just thinking how much it must be annoying my ex-fiancé that she has lost a Duke."

"You said that before," William replied, "and, as I hear she now has two sons, I think for the moment at any rate that she is nearer to the winning post than you."

"Two sons!" the Duke exclaimed before he could prevent himself.

Then he shrugged his shoulders.

"She is welcome to them and so is her husband. Personally I prefer my freedom and it is my freedom I wish to keep, not only now but as long as I live."

William chuckled and then he said,

"We have had this conversation before and I would suggest that it's banned in the future. Let's consider what camera I will buy tomorrow morning and which brand is most likely to take the best photographs."

"I have never taken that much interest in them," the Duke said. "It's extraordinary to me that the Queen is so obsessed by photographs that her sitting room is filled with pictures of her children and, of course, the much lamented Prince Albert."

"Are you suggesting that we should ask the Queen where to buy the best camera so you can display yourself and your supposed bride?"

"I cannot for the moment think of anyone else who is particularly keen on photography," the Duke answered. "What I should do, William, is to buy a camera which is recommended for a non-professional for the taking of the best photographs and make it clear to the man in the shop that, if it is not good, you will demand your money back."

"I am not likely to get that. At the same time I don't want you to be disappointed. I saw some photographs of some of my relatives the other day that were absolutely appalling. In fact, it was difficult to recognise them."

"All that really matters is to show the gown and that it is worn by a woman with me standing beside her. No one in the wilds of the Caucasus is likely to ask too many questions about my wife."

He paused a moment, then declared firmly,

"I simply have to convince Prince Vladimir that I am a married man and so unavailable as a son-in-law."

He stopped short and then added,

"It has suddenly struck me, William, why has he not thought of you? After all, your father was a rich man who owned a large amount of land."

"Yes, but he did not have a title and it's a title that matters on the Continent and a great deal in Mayfair as well!"

William laughed as he continued,

"Stop trying to pull the wool over my eyes, John. You know as well as I do that the *debutantes* and their mothers have been running after you like a lot of silly sheep ever since you came into your title. In fact, the number of invitations you receive is phenomenal."

"That is exactly what I find disgusting about the whole thing," the Duke replied. "Women marry for what they can get out of it, and the prettier the girl is, the higher she expects to rise in *Debrett's Peerage*. If I was not good enough for them when I was plain Mr. Ford, I am certainly not going to marry a woman now just because she wants to be a Duchess."

William sighed.

"The trouble with you John, is that because you have been done down by one woman, you are now making yourself hate the whole sex. There is good and bad in females, just as there is in males and you were unfortunate to pick a bad one."

"Exactly, and once bitten, twice shy. That is why, William, I will never be the bridegroom, except when I pose for you for a photograph!"

He left the room as he finished speaking and, as the door closed behind him, William sighed again.

He was very fond of his friend and enjoyed being with him.

But at the same time he regretted that, because one woman had insulted him and made him feel foolish, he insisted on condemning them all. It was spoiling him and his chance of happiness for the future.

'I expect some day he will get over it,' William told himself.

But he was not confident that was possible.

CHAPTER THREE

After they had enjoyed an excellent luncheon at the Ducal house in Berkeley Square, the Duke and William climbed into the chaise and they set off at a good speed.

The Duke thought with satisfaction that William had purchased a splendid if expensive camera.

It would be impossible for anyone in Georgia not to believe he was married if he showed them a photograph of him and his wife in that magnificent wedding dress.

He had remembered to instruct his valet to put his evening clothes and his father's decorations in the chaise.

He wanted to add those that had belonged to the previous Duke, but unfortunately most of them were in the safe at the family castle in Scotland.

However, he had been a Knight of the Order of the Garter and the Duke was able to add that insignia to his Collection, even though no one in Georgia would know what the Garter meant, but it would certainly look impressive.

He was, in fact, enjoying himself in thinking out new ideas for circumventing those who continually nagged him to be married and he knew that it was now going to be worse than it had ever been simply because, as a Duke, he would require an heir.

Thinking it over, he was quite certain that there were a few relations who could claim the Dukedom when he was dead, which he hoped would not be for a long time.

As they reached the outskirts of London, the Duke gave the horses their heads and they moved quickly down the empty roads.

"I do see there is one advantage," the Duke said, "in living near London. You can get out into the country without having to travel for miles as I have to do when I go to The Castle."

"I agree with you that Sutherland is a long distance to travel every time you want to go home," William said. "If I ever have a country estate, which is very unlikely, it will be in what is known as 'the Home Counties'."

They travelled on and William asked,

"What is this girl like who you are making your alleged wife?"

"She is very pretty, in fact, outstandingly so. I can hardly be accused of marrying an ugly woman!"

"No, of course not, John, but you don't think she may blackmail you in the future because she has pretended to be your wife?"

"Good heavens, no! After all Charles, although a spendthrift, was undoubtedly a gentleman. I remember my father talking warmly of Lord Lester."

"I was only making sure that you are safe."

The Duke smiled.

"You are quite right, William. It would be a great mistake to take any risks and that is why I am determined to make absolutely clear from the very beginning that I am not available as a husband for the Princess."

He paused before he added,

"In fact, it was you who made me aware that it would be very foolish to go to Georgia as a bachelor."

"Very foolish indeed," William agreed. "I only hope now that the photographs are really convincing."

"That is up to you, William."

"I have never at any time pretended to be a skilled photographer. In point of fact, my photographs have not been particularly good and I am only hoping that with this new and very expensive camera I will be more successful."

"I will be extremely annoyed if you are not," the Duke said, "and it will be embarrassing if we have to ask Miss Lester to do it all over again."

"The man in the shop assured me it was foolproof, but I don't think I could earn my living as a photographer."

They both laughed at this.

Three quarters of an hour later they were driving in at the gates of The Hermitage and, when they came within sight of the house, William gave an exclamation.

"I had no idea it was so attractive. What a lovely house! No wonder the owner does not want to sell it."

"Apparently it has been in the Lester family for years and I agree with you that it must be heartbreaking to have to sell it just to pay for Charles's extravagance."

They drew up outside the front door and the groom, who had been sitting behind them, jumped down to go to the horses' heads.

"We will be some time, Jenkins," the Duke said to the man. "If you would like to take the horses round to the stable yard, you can do so. But I doubt if you will find anyone to help you."

"I'll manage, Your Grace," Jenkins replied.

The Duke walked up to the front door to find that it was already open and Brooks was bowing politely.

"Good afternoon, Your Grace," he intoned. "Miss Alnina has asked me to show you into the music room and she'll join you as soon as she's ready."

"I have to change my clothes first," the Duke said, "and my friend, Mr. Armstrong, is carrying the case."

Brooks bent forward to take it from William and, as he put it down on the floor, he said,

"Perhaps Your Grace would like to see the music room first. Then I'll take you upstairs, so that Your Grace can change into what you'll be wearing."

"Thank you," the Duke replied.

Brooks led the way down the same passage where the Duke had been before when he went to the study.

At the far end there were double doors, which he had not noticed when he was touring the rest of the house with Alnina.

Brooks opened both the doors and the Duke saw that, what had been the music room, which had doubtless also served as a ballroom, ran the whole length of that side of the house and long windows opened onto the garden.

It had originally been painted white picked out in gold, but the white had darkened in many places and the gold had faded.

But Alnina had arranged a mass of flowers at one end of the room with most of them white, as was suitable for a wedding.

On the wall there was a very beautiful mirror with a carved frame and one glance at it told the Duke that it was a perfect background for a bride and bridegroom.

He sensed that William was thinking the same, but he did not say so as Brooks was still with them.

"The gentleman can easily put up his camera here," Brooks said, "and Miss Alnina was certain that this would be the background Your Grace required for the picture."

"Yes, indeed," the Duke affirmed. "And we are most grateful to have it."

"Now, if Your Grace'll come with me," Brooks asked, "I'll take Your Grace upstairs."

The Duke followed him, noticing as he did so, how much furniture had clearly disappeared from the corridors and how many pictures were missing on the walls.

He had only been vaguely interested when Alnina had taken him round the house for the first time, but now, because she was helping him, he told himself, he must do his best to help her.

He was very certain that many of his friends and acquaintances were keen to collect genuine antiques.

'I must tell them about the items that are for sale,' he told himself. 'Then I am sure she will be able to pay off Charles's debts.'

He was shown by Brooks into what he recognised was the Master bedroom.

In this room was a rather uncomfortably large bed with its velvet canopy and the family insignia embroidered over the headboard.

There was also an extremely fine chest of drawers which Lord Lester had used as a dressing table and over it there was an impressive gold mirror with the family crest on top of it.

Brooks had placed his suitcase on a chair and was taking out the evening clothes which he laid neatly on the bed and the medals he put on the chest of drawers.

The Duke took off his coat and trousers and it did not take him long to replace them with satin breeches and silk stockings.

When he was finally dressed and wearing the blue Order of the Garter across his chest, he thought he certainly looked the part.

Undoubtedly any foreigner would be impressed and only an Englishman would know he was overdressed and his clothes were more suitable for a dinner at Buckingham Palace than a wedding in the country.

"I'll find Miss Alnina, Your Grace, and tell her that you're ready," Brooks offered.

"Thank you and I would expect my friend is also ready with his camera."

Brooks disappeared and the Duke, after another glance at himself in the mirror, walked down the passage.

Once again he was realising what a large number of pictures had gone from the walls.

As he reached the hall, he was aware, as he had not been before, that it was empty of chairs, tables and also, he suspected a grandfather clock.

At the end of the passage, he met Brooks coming back from the music room.

"Miss Alnina's there, Your Grace," he said.

The Duke walked on and through the open door into the music room.

Alnina was standing at the far end of it in front of the flowers.

The Duke thought even at a first glance that she looked lovelier than any woman he had ever seen.

She had taken a great deal of trouble in putting on the amazingly decorative wedding dress. It was just as she thought her mother must have worn it all those years ago.

She had found the wedding veil, which had been in the family for years. It had taken her some time and the wreath of white roses on her head was exquisitely made and exceedingly becoming.

She only had a small necklace of her own pearls to wear round her neck, as her mother had worn a diamond necklace.

It made Alnina look young and more beautiful than if she had been loaded down by too many jewels.

There were quite enough on the dress and it was shining in the sun pouring in through the open windows.

With the background of flowers she looked, the Duke thought as he walked towards her, as if she had just stepped out of a Fairy tale.

William had by now set up his camera.

As the Duke took Alnina's hand in his, William thought that it would be impossible to find a more good-looking pair anywhere in the world.

Although he did not say so, he thought they must have stepped out of a dream and could not be real flesh and blood.

"Thank you for all the trouble you have taken," the Duke was saying.

"I hope you are pleased, Your Grace. I was afraid that there would not be enough flowers for the background you required. But I found them in the end even though it was a somewhat lengthy search."

The Duke smiled.

"No one," he said, "will look at the background when they can look at you."

"I hope that you are right. My wreath was another formidable task, but I managed it and I also made myself a bouquet."

"You have thought of everything and I cannot tell you how grateful I am."

"Now let's get on with the photographs," William said. "I am sure the sun is giving us exactly the right light and you never know when it might go behind a cloud."

"Heaven forbid!" the Duke exclaimed. "The sooner you photograph us the better."

He moved quickly in front of the flowers.

Then Alnina said a little shyly,

"Do you think I should put my hand on your arm?"

"Yes, of course. And I should have thought of that myself. If we had only just been married, we would hardly stand far apart from each other."

"It all depends who you married," Alnina replied. "But I think, as you are so smart, and I must commend you on your decorations, they would expect us to look happy and be quite near to each other."

"Yes, of course," the Duke agreed.

He stood with his back to the flowers and Alnina put her hand on his arm, holding her bouquet with the other one.

It was only when he had looked through his lens that William gave a cry.

"You have forgotten something," he cautioned.

"What is that?" the Duke asked.

"The bride is showing her left hand and there is no ring on it."

"How stupid of me!" Alnina cried. "I had thought of it. I have Mama's ring upstairs, but I forgot to put it on my finger."

The Duke took off his signet ring.

"If you turn this round the other way," he said, "it will save your going upstairs or sending your man to fetch it for you."

"Of course. I told him we were doing this to show abroad how people dress for balls at Buckingham Palace. So we were quite right to make it look glamorous."

"What about your veil?" the Duke asked.

"Your friend will tell you I put it on after Brooks left the room," Alnina said. "All he saw was the wreath and after all a great number of women wear a wreath when they don't have a tiara."

The Duke laughed.

"That is very true. But what woman does not prefer diamonds to flowers?"

"I for one. I love flowers and, although I admire diamonds, I cannot say I love them."

"Then you are indeed unique. I have never known a woman who did not wish to cover herself with gems and who did not prefer to wear something that glittered rather than flowers that scent the air."

"Now if you will both stop talking like characters on the stage at Drury Lane," William piped up. "I want to get this photograph taken."

"It is my fault we have been delayed," Alnina said. "I should have remembered the ring. It was clever of you to notice it."

"Now smile and look happy," William ordered and then he was peering into his camera.

They heard the clicks as he took several exposures.

Then he suggested, as he pulled off the velvet hood that covered his head,

"I think we should have one now with you looking at each other."

"Do you think that is really necessary?" the Duke enquired.

"I think it is a wise move to make it clear that your heart is in England, even if your body is walking about in Georgia."

"All right then, but hurry up. If there is one thing I really dislike, it's being photographed."

"Don't think of it like that," Alnina said. "This is a theatrical performance and we have to make it a success!"

She paused for a moment before she added,

"Otherwise you may be sorry you have bought the wedding dress."

"I will be delighted to add it to the collection of robes of every type in the family mansion," he asserted. "There is a whole room full of them, but none are as fine or as beautiful as your wedding dress, Miss Lester."

"I am glad to hear that," Alnina said. "It is exactly the sort of home I want it to have, because my mother was so proud of it."

"That is not surprising. It certainly is unique and my only trouble is that it will attract a great number of my family who will all want to come and stay with me."

The Duke laughed before he added,

"Not because they find me charming, but because I have such a beautiful wedding dress for which they will try to persuade me to find a bride!"

"That should not be difficult!" Alnina responded.

"Let me tell you it is impossible, because I intend never to marry anyone. I have an uncomfortable feeling it will make those who continually pester me that much more voluble than they are already."

"I am not surprised. All Dukes need to leave an heir behind them."

"Oh, there will be plenty of those," the Duke said. "The only difference is that they will not be my sons."

There was silence for a moment and

Then Alnina said,

"I think that is rather sad."

"Now come on," William interrupted. "All I want you to do is to look at each other and appear loving, even though you feel that this is a confounded bore."

Alnina laughed and turned to the Duke,

"Mr. Armstrong is quite right. We should get down to business and I will look up at you affectionately."

She threw back her head as she spoke.

As the Duke looked down at her, he thought that it would be very difficult to find another woman anywhere in the world who was quite so attractive.

'What I have to do,' he thought, 'because I knew Charles and because she has been so kind to me is to find her a really nice husband. I just wonder if she would fancy William?'

"Now," said William, almost as if the Duke had spoken his thoughts aloud, "don't move and for Heaven's sake look affectionate."

The Duke bent his head a little nearer to Alnina.

She stared up at him.

Their eyes met and then she felt a little feeling run through her that she had never felt before.

They both stood very still, almost as if mesmerised.

William once again threw off the velvet cloth and declared,

"Excellent! Really excellent! If it does not come out exactly as you looked, I will be furious and sue the man who sold me the camera!"

"I am sure it will be perfect," the Duke said. "Now if you have finished, I will go and change."

"And I will do the same," Alnina added. "Then I am sure that Brooks has tea ready for us all in the study."

"I will look forward to that," William said. "I think I deserve it after all the trouble I have had in taking these photographs."

"It has been far worse for us," the Duke protested. "After all, we have had to dress up and obey commands.

And that is something I have managed to avoid up to now, even though we have known each other for years."

"That is certainly true enough," William replied. "You always think that you know best, so I have given up arguing with you."

The Duke laughed and countered,

"I have not noticed much difference."

"Perhaps you will in the future. Now ostensibly you are a married man and I have proof of it!"

"You are scaring me, William, and before you say any more I am going upstairs to change and be again, as I have always been and always intend to be, a very sensible bachelor without a heart."

He had left the room before William could answer.

Alnina, who had been putting her bouquet in water so that the flowers would not die, turned round.

"Why is your friend, the Duke, so determined not to marry?" she asked him. "And everyone will expect him to, although I quite understand that he has no wish to marry this Princess from another country."

William glanced at the door, almost as if he felt the Duke was still there listening to him.

"He was very badly treated by someone he loved and whom he had asked to marry him," he said. "But don't tell him I have told you so."

"Oh, how sad! Did she jilt him?"

"Yes, she did and only a few days before they were due to be married."

Alnina stared at him.

"How terrible! How could she do such a thing?"

"She did it because she wanted a title. She married instead a Viscount who will become an Earl. Little did she know, if she had waited long enough, she would have been a Duchess."

Alnina was silent for a moment and then she said,

"I suppose many women would think it important. Yet when they marry it should be the man himself who counts and not that he has or has not a title to his name."

"If they are honest," William replied, "most women dream that a Duke will drop down the chimney and ask them to be his wife. They are therefore disappointed when he is just Mr. Snooks or Captain Know-all!"

Alnina laughed.

"You are funny, but it's true. Yet I don't believe that all women are so avaricious."

As William was silent, she went on,

"Personally I think that if I was married to someone very grand, it would be such a bore to entertain people who came not because they were real friends, but because they wanted to say they had dined with the Duke of 'This' or the Earl of 'That'."

William was amused and responded,

"You are different from most people. But I have never found a woman yet who was not anxious to have a title and go into dinner in front of her friends."

"Well, now you have met me," Alnina said. "I can assure you that when I marry it will not be because the man in question is important, even if he is the King of Sheba. It will be because I love him and he loves me."

"That is exactly what you should feel, but I cannot believe that dressed up as you are now you will not expect a God from Olympus or perhaps an archangel from Heaven to be kneeling at your feet."

Alnina walked towards the door, saying,

"Now you are putting ideas into my head. So I am going to change and just be a plain young woman who has no aspirations beyond paying her brother's debts."

She had gone before William could think of a reply, but he was chuckling as he packed up his camera.

He was reflecting that Miss Lester was far more amusing than most young women he had met and she was certainly different from any *debutantes* who giggled when he spoke to them and had nothing to say for themselves.

*

The Duke came down first and found William in the study.

"I hope," he said, "those pictures are good. You have certainly taken a great deal of trouble over them."

"They will be fantastic. I can promise you that. I will have them developed and printed off by the day after tomorrow."

"Then we can start to make our plans as to when we can leave for Georgia," the Duke said with satisfaction.

"There is one thing that is worrying me, John."

"What is that, William?"

"If you really buy this mountain on which you have set your heart, how are you going to give your orders to the men who will be working for you?"

The Duke looked at him.

"What do you mean by that?" he asked.

"Well, neither of us speaks Russian and, although the Prince speaks French, as do all aristocratic Russians, the workers will speak only Russian and not particularly cultured Russian at that."

"I suppose I will have an overseer and someone in charge who will give them their orders," the Duke replied.

"And, of course, once it has been organised, you and I can go back to England or anywhere else we fancy and merely pick up the gold on our return."

"That all sounds very easy, but you know that in Georgia, as in Russia, you cannot trust anyone unless you are there yourself giving the orders."

He saw that the Duke was listening and went on,

"You are going to find it hard to find an overseer who is honest and also speaks French and will not put your gold into his own pocket."

There was silence and then the Duke said,

"You always produce the most irritating stumbling blocks when I least expect them. Of course you are right, but I suppose with my usual good luck I will find someone I can trust and hope for the best."

"If you ask me, that is not good enough," William answered. "Before we go and buy this ridiculous mountain you have set your heart on, we must both learn Russian."

The Duke laughed.

"I wonder how long it would take us. It's the most ghastly language I have met on my travels. If you recall, when we were in Tiflis before, you complained that, unless we were conversing with the High and Mighty, you never understood a word that was said to you."

"That is exactly what I am saying to you now."

They were walking along the passage and came to the study where Brooks was holding the door open.

"Tea is ready, Your Grace," he said to the Duke, "and I do hope you enjoys the cake my Missus has made especially for you."

"That is very kind of her. Please thank her. I am sure it will be delicious."

"I hope that you'll say the same when your Grace's eaten it," Brooks replied.

The two men went into the study where Alnina was sitting on the sofa.

She was looking, the Duke thought, exceedingly attractive in a cotton dress, which might not have been the height of fashion, but it matched the blue of her eyes.

"Come and have tea," she said. "You deserve it. I heard Brooks telling you that his wife has made one of her special cakes and she will be hurt and upset if you don't enjoy it."

"I am sure that it's like everything else you have given us," the Duke said, "unique and different in every way from anything we have had before."

Alnina laughed.

"I am so glad that is my reputation, because like you I get very bored when things are humdrum and always exactly the same. That is why I like travelling."

"I have just been telling the Duke," William said, "that it will be no use his impressing Prince Vladimir with our photographs if we cannot find an honest overseer for the mountain."

Even as he finished speaking, he realised that he had been indiscreet and the Duke had not told Alnina what he was trying to buy from the Prince.

He put his fingers up to his lips and, looking at the Duke, sighed,

"I am sorry, John."

"I thought that it was women who could not keep a secret," the Duke said. "But I feel that we can trust Miss Lester, so we will let her into the plan."

"Oh, please do!" Alnina begged. "You told me that there was a special reason for your going to Georgia, but not what it was."

"The trouble with William has always been that he talks too much, but our secret, now that you know at least a quarter of it, shall be yours and I will tell you that, ever since I last visited Georgia and saw the fantastic Caucasus mountains, I wanted to own one."

Alnina stared at him.

"To own a mountain! But how exciting! And how thrilling! Of course it would be something really precious to have, all of one's own."

"That is exactly what I feel, but I never thought that I could possibly afford one until by the curious hand of Fate I became the Duke."

"Now you are really going to buy a mountain? It's the most intriguing idea I have ever heard."

"Everyone else will think I am a fool, but this is the one thing I want, because, when William and I were there some years ago, we explored one that belongs to Prince Vladimir and we are quite certain that it contains gold."

"So then you will have a gold mountain all of your own. It's not surprising that you are so excited."

"William has just presented a difficulty however."

"What is that?" Alnina asked.

"Well, neither of us speak Russian and, as he has pointed out, we will need to hire a trustworthy overseer we can give orders to. We must hope that he speaks French."

Alnina looked from one to the other.

"Are you really telling me that you are thinking of buying a mountain which will cost you a lot of money and neither of you speaks Russian?"

"Because we both spoke French all the time with the people we were staying with and with the Prince when we met him, it never occurred to me that the ordinary people of Georgia speak a different language altogether."

"But of course they do," Alnina said.

"What I have suggested," William broke in, "is that we both learn Russian before we go out and spend a great deal of money buying this mountain over which, however much gold it contains, we are bound to be crooked."

"I think that is very likely, Alnina remarked, but it will take you some time. It took me a year to learn Russian and I had one of the best teachers ever."

The Duke stared at her.

"You speak Russian?"

"Fluently, I am glad to say," Alnina replied. "But I did work very hard at it and, as I had completed all the other lessons in the school, I did nothing else."

There was silence for a moment and then William said,

"Then of course you will have to teach us."

Alnina smiled.

"For one year? Or if you enjoy your life in London, which undoubtedly you do, it might be two or three years."

Again there was silence before the Duke suggested,

"The only possible answer to this problem is that you come out with us to Georgia. Then you can give the overseer his orders and we hope that he passes them on."

"Are you serious?" Alnina enquired.

"Of course I am serious. I have been dreaming of this for years. Now that it is actually within my reach to own a mountain that seems to me much more exciting than anything else I have seen on my travels, I just cannot give up and admit I am defeated."

"No, of course not, but I am sure that you could find someone more suitable than I am."

The Duke spread out his hands.

"Quite frankly we know no one. And to go to the Russian Embassy would be crazy."

"Why should it be?" William enquired.

"Don't be silly. You know as well as I do, if the Russians thought that there was gold in the mountain you are talking about, the gold would be theirs before we even left home."

"Mr. Armstrong is absolutely right there," Alnina agreed. "The Russians, I was told by my teacher, who was a Russian, have been actively searching for gold and every other available mineral in the Caucasus."

She smiled at them both before she continued,

"But those who prospected in the North have often been disappointed. And they have now almost given up believing that treasure is there waiting for them."

They looked at each other and then William said,

"Miss Lester is quite right. I think, if she will come with us to Tiflis, it will make those we meet think we are merely on an adventurous holiday."

"That is sheer common sense," the Duke said, "so please, Miss Lester, or rather Alnina – remember I knew your brother and please call me John – will you come with us as my guest and help me buy the one possession I really want to own?"

"It is the most exciting invitation I have ever had," Alnina enthused, "but how can I leave everything here with Charles's creditors trying every way they can to extract money from me that I do not have?"

"You can leave all that in the hands of my Solicitor and one of my Managers," the Duke said. "Most of them have little to do at The Castle as they have already made it almost perfect. My Solicitor will keep the dogs at bay until you return."

"I cannot believe you are really serious about this," Alnina sighed.

"I am completely serious and William will tell you how much I have longed for this particular mountain, but have never been rich enough until now to buy an inch of it, let alone the whole mountain itself."

Alnina looked from one to the other.

"I don't know what to say. You have taken all my breath away and I cannot think clearly."

"Just leave it all to me. I will arrange that nothing difficult happens while you are away and, if the creditors get really out of hand, my people shall pay them and we can then discuss later how much you owe me instead of them."

"I feel breathless," Alnina murmured. "Of course it will be thrilling for me to go to Georgia and to see the Caucasus. It is something I thought would never actually happen and I would only be able to read about it, as I have done already, in books."

"Very well. William and I will go back to London and I will send down one of my Managers and a Solicitor tomorrow for you to give them your instructions as to what is to be sold in the house and what is not."

The Duke smiled at her.

"Personally," he went on, "I think it would be best if nothing was sold until we return."

"I doubt if the creditors will agree to that," Alnina answered in a small voice.

"Very well, they will just have to be paid off," the Duke asserted.

He then looked up at the empty space over the mantelpiece and continued,

"I only wish that this had happened sooner and you would have been able to keep a great number of pictures that you have already sold."

"I hated doing it," Alnina admitted, "and it would have broken Papa's heart."

"Well, what is done cannot be undone," the Duke said. "But we can make amends for you in the future and, as our teacher, you will be entitled to a large salary."

Alnina stared at him incredulously.

"Are you really serious?" she asked.

"Of course I am. It matters to me enormously. I am not so concerned with money, but only with possessing the mountain I have always wanted and, if you like, loved as if it was the wife everyone is begging me to marry."

William laughed.

"You would find it cold, hard and cumbersome when you were making love to it!"

"Now you are just being unpleasant, William. The mountain is what I dream about and I have wanted it ever since we first saw it. Now I have a chance of making it mine I am not going to miss it. That is my final word, so it is no use arguing with me about it."

"I would not dare," William said. "I just know how pig-headed you can be when you make up your mind and Alnina will have to get used to that, just as I have."

Alnina was looking from one to the other as if she could not believe that what they were saying was true.

Then the Duke announced,

"With any luck we will leave next week. Now tell me if there is anything else you want done while we are away."

"I hate to say it, but Brooks and his wife have been wonderful to me and have looked after me ever since I was a baby. They have hardly been able to afford enough food when we have not sold anything and they have not been paid any wages for months."

"You can leave that to me," the Duke said.

"I hate to bother you with it," Alnina replied, "but they are the only people who have helped me since I have been alone."

"As I have already said," the Duke insisted, "I will see that the Brookses are cared for and have help in the house while you are away with me."

"Oh, thank you! Thank you!" Alnina cried. "I just could not bear them being half-starved, as they have been at times and I am sure that they would feel very lonely in the house if there was no one with them."

"I will see that Mrs. Brooks has someone to help in the kitchen and that Brooks has a footman."

Alnina threw up her hands.

"I don't believe it. I am dreaming all this and will wake up and find that I am alone in bed."

"You will wake up and find that you are in Tiflis and have a thousand things to do for me," the Duke said. "Before we leave I am certain that, as my wife, you will want some fashionable and expensive clothes as part of my bargain."

He paused before he added,

"You had better come to London and stay two or three nights and buy what you want, which, of course, must be suitable for a Duchess."

Alnina drew in her breath.

"Now I am quite certain that I will wake up at any moment!" she exclaimed.

"In that case William and I are going to leave while you convince yourself you have not been dreaming and are merely being practical! And, of course, earning your salary as our teacher and, as far as Tiflis is concerned, as my wife!"

Alnina then stared at him again as if she could not believe what she was hearing, but William laughed.

"This is John all over! Once he gets going there is no stopping him. So come along, John, it is time we went back to London and you can send a carriage for Alnina tomorrow morning."

"You are quite right, William, because we have so much to do. Goodbye, Alnina, and remember that you are doing me the kindest turn ever and I am extremely grateful to you."

He shook her hand.

Then, as he was unable to speak for the moment, he walked ahead out of the door with William behind him.

By the time Alnina had followed them to the front door, they were already climbing into the chaise.

"So we will see you tomorrow," the Duke shouted, waving his hand.

Then, as the horses moved off, Alnina stopped at the top of the steps and with difficulty waved back.

'This cannot be true, I am dreaming, I know I am dreaming,' she sighed to herself, as she walked very slowly back to the study.

CHAPTER FOUR

The very next morning Alnina was astonished when two men arrived, sent by the Duke.

One was a Solicitor, the other one of his Managers.

"His Grace has told us," they informed her, "that we are to look after your estate and keep Lord Lester's creditors at bay until you return with him from his trip."

Brooks had shown them into the study.

Alnina was there at the writing table making notes of what would be required.

She could not help feeling that it might all be a hoax. She was genuinely afraid that His Grace would, at the last moment, change his mind and not take her.

Now she realised that everything had to be done in a hurry and she produced the collection of bills that had not been paid.

To her intense relief the Solicitor did not exclaim with horror, but took them quietly into his possession and he assured her that there would be no trouble while she was abroad.

It was more difficult to explain to the Manager what was required on the estate and that she was trying to save the pensioners from starving and to keep the land in a reasonably good condition without spending too much.

"The sad truth is," she said, "I don't have any at the moment. You can readily understand that, although I have managed to sell many items, I still have to find even more for the creditors before spending anything on the estate."

She gave a deep sigh before she added,

"At the same time I cannot allow people to starve simply because I cannot give them what my father did and my grandfather before him."

"I understand," the Manager said. "His Grace has told me that I am to do the best I can for your people and that he will supply anything urgently needed while you are away.

"It is *so* kind of him," Alnina smiled.

However, she felt ashamed that she should have to accept what was really charity from a stranger and her only consolation was that the Duke and William had known Charles at Eton.

Therefore they had been to some extent friends of his and so she did have some tie with them.

Almost before she had finished telling the Manager about the estate, a carriage arrived to take her to London.

It was drawn by two horses and it was the kind of carriage that she imagined her mother driving about in.

It was certainly one they could not afford after she was born and her father had begun to find that things were more expensive than they had been.

Mrs. Brooks had helped her pack everything she thought she would need and she could not help wondering if the Duke had been serious when he had told her that he would provide her with the smart clothes she should wear if she was in fact a Duchess.

She was not ready to leave until very late in the afternoon, as she had so much to tell the Manager.

It was only when he and the Solicitor left that she finally said goodbye to the Brookses.

"You will look after yourselves and the house while I am away," she instructed Brooks.

"Now don't worry, Miss Alnina. That gentleman gives us the good news that we're to have our wages and there'll be food for us to eat. No one could ask for more, especially when he says the Missus is to have help in the kitchen and I'm to have a footman."

He laughed.

"It's so long since I'd had a footman, I thinks I've forgotten how to teach him."

"I am sure that you will remember once you have chosen one," Alnina said consolingly.

"Now all you has to do," Brooks went on, "is to enjoy yourself while you're away. I thinks His Grace be a real gentleman and no one can say more."

"Of course not," Alnina agreed.

She kissed Mrs. Brooks goodbye and shook hands with Brooks.

Then she climbed into the carriage and waved from the window as it drove off down the drive.

'Can this really happening to me and it's not just a dream?' she thought as she passed the dilapidated gates.

All the way to London she found herself thinking how exciting it all was and she was checking in her mind that she had not forgotten anything.

When she finally arrived at the very grand house in Berkeley Square, it was to find that the Duke and William were waiting for her.

"The photographs are wonderful," William began. "The printer did them for me today and they are here for you to see."

He had them spread out on a table and Alnina had to admit they looked as a bride and bridegroom should, but, of course, very much more elegant than any wedding couple she had ever seen before.

Then, as she was looking at them, a sudden thought made her glance up at the Duke and ask,

"Are you showing me these to tell me that after all you will not need me on your trip to Tiflis?"

The Duke smiled.

"Only if you can promise me that the photographs, which I agree are excellent, can speak Russian!"

Alnina gave a little sigh of relief.

"I am afraid that's not possible, so you will have to put up with me, John."

"That is exactly what we intend to do," the Duke said. "I have been talking it all over with William, and we have decided it would be far more comfortable to travel by sea than overland."

Alnina was listening excitedly, but did not interrupt and he therefore went on,

"I am hiring a large yacht, as, although I have been intending to buy one myself, I have not yet done so. My predecessor and his sons were drowned in a boat, which he always used. It was very old and he should have replaced it at least five or six years before it destroyed him."

"Then what have you hired?" Alnina asked.

"I have fortunately discovered that it is very easy to hire a yacht from an owner who does not use it very often. I have found the Marquis of Templeton, who won a prize at Cowes last year, is only too pleased to rent me his yacht as long as it is back in England in time for Cowes Week."

"And will we be back by then?" William asked.

"I have no intention of staying away from home longer than I can possibly help. When I am exploring, I never linger long, as some men do, in one place."

"Then you have this yacht available now?" Alnina asked, as she felt that they should keep to the point.

"It will be waiting in the Thames for us the day after tomorrow and by that time you should have managed to buy your trousseau."

Alnina laughed.

"Most women would scream at being given so little time. But, as I am not really entitled to a trousseau, I shall be very grateful for anything I have time to buy and I will not keep you waiting."

"I will be very disagreeable if you do," the Duke said. "I have made a success of my life so far by always being on time and never prevaricating, as so many people do at the last moment, changing their minds when it is least expected."

Alnina looked at him.

"I wonder why," she asked, "you are so precise about everything. Was it because you were brought up that way or is it a rebellion against people who were sloppy and annoyed you as soon as you were old enough to understand what was happening?"

"That is a very intelligent question and the answer is both. I remember my father being exceedingly precise and people so often had to sympathise with him when my mother constantly changed her mind at the last moment."

The Duke smiled at her.

"It might have been a party she was giving, which she would suddenly decide to postpone to a week later or she would want to change her dress when the carriage was already waiting to take them to a ball."

Alnina laughed.

"I can imagine that being extremely annoying to any man. Perhaps the woman you ought to marry, but have no

70

intention of doing so, is lucky because she has escaped being lectured every time she irritated you."

"I am making it clear to you as my supposed wife," the Duke asserted, "that I expect you to be on time. In fact, as William will tell you, I am most disagreeable when and if anyone keeps me waiting, even the dogs."

"Well, I imagine they at least, will not be with us and I promise I will do my very best not to upset you in any way."

She looked so pretty as she spoke that the Duke could not help thinking that it would be easy to forgive her, even if she was a culprit.

He was now arranging where she should go for her shopping the next day.

He was certain that she had never entered any of the Bond Street shops himself, but luckily he had a good idea which were the favourite shops of the smartest ladies.

He pointed out that, as they expected everything to be ready in only a few hours, what Alnina bought would certainly be more expensive than if she had more time.

"I will try to get everything that fits me and does not have to be altered," Alnina said. "And I can sew very well myself and I am sure I could alter any dress which required only a little to be done to it."

"I am beginning to feel rather nervous about all the things you can do. I quite expect you to tell me at any moment that you can navigate the yacht if the Captain is taken ill and you will also cook for us if the French chef I have engaged does not turn up!"

"You make me sound terrible," Alnina replied. "I hate pushy, bossy women and I am sure you do too. So I promise to be neither of those things and only obedient to your gracious command!"

She saluted him as she spoke and William clapped his hands.

"No one could possibly say more!" he exclaimed. "You know that you love being Monarch of all you survey, John, and here we are down on our knees in front of you."

"Quite right too," the Duke said. "After all, this is my campaign and I am determined that it will be a great success."

*

They set off two days later after breakfast.

The yacht, which was very large, was, in Alnina's eyes, the most enchanting ship she had ever seen.

She had once been with her father on board a much smaller yacht and when she was quite young she had been taken down the Thames. It was in a boat that had been hired by some friends of her mother as a birthday treat.And so Alnina had not enjoyed herself as much as she had hoped she would.

But now the Duke had managed to find a yacht that was larger and more luxurious than any she had ever seen.

They were piped grandly aboard and welcomed by the Captain.

He introduced his Officers and they also met the three Stewards who would attend to them on the voyage and the Duke insisted on meeting the chef.

Then, as they began to move slowly down the River Thames, Alnina thought again that this could not really be happening to her.

Later they explored the yacht and, when she was shown into her luxurious cabin, she found that the Duke's valet, Albert, had unpacked her clothes for her.

Afterwards she said rather shyly, because she was not certain how her suggestion would be received,

"I think, John, that you and William should allow me to teach you some Russian while we are sailing towards Georgia."

For a moment both the men were too surprised to answer and then the Duke enquired,

"Are you really suggesting we should have lessons from you as your pupils?"

"You will find it far more convenient to be able to speak even a little Russian yourself than to rely on me for every word," Alnina replied.

He did not answer and she went on,

"I often thought that if I have to earn my own living I might become a teacher of children, or better still, teach Russian, French or any European language in a school."

"It certainly seems a good idea – "

The Duke looked at William as he spoke.

"I should be delighted," William said, "to learn Russian from such a charming and attractive teacher. I can only hope that I will prove a clever pupil who will do you credit."

The Duke chuckled.

"Well, after that what can I say except 'yes'! But you must not be too severe with us. I like being at sea and I enjoy being on the bridge more than anything else."

"I can understand that but then your education must come first and I promise you, although it is a very difficult language, it will be an asset when we arrive."

"Of course it will," William said, "and we must insist that John attends to his lessons. I have a feeling he will dislike it if I beat him!"

"I have to be first in everything, as you well know," the Duke answered. "I must make sure that Alnina points me out as her best and most promising pupil!"

Because she had anticipated that they would, when she was not actually teaching them, ask her a number of questions, she had been sensible enough to bring with her a few books on Russia and text books on the language.

Some of them she had used when she was learning it herself and, when she told the Duke and William what she had done, they said that it was very thoughtful of her.

"But," the Duke said, "today is a holiday and I refuse to have any meals spoilt by being told how I should pronounce food in Russian, which I have always thought was a very ugly language."

"Not as ugly as German, but you are quite right and we will start our lessons tomorrow morning. I think they should take at least two hours every day. And perhaps you should do some homework on memorising vocabulary."

She smiled at them both.

"Then when you reach Tiflis," she went on, "you will be able to give your orders to the servants in Russian and also, of course, to the overseer of your mountain."

"When it really becomes yours," William muttered.

"I will look forward to that," the Duke replied. "Now let's talk of more interesting subjects."

"I have hardly had time yet," Alnina said, "to read much about Georgia. But, as you know, the Caucasians were always particularly dangerous fighting men."

"Worse than from other parts of Russia?" William asked.

"Yes, indeed. In one book I was reading it said that the Caucasians wrote love poems to their daggers."

The two men laughed.

"I hope we will not do that," the Duke said, "when I become a Caucasian proprietor."

"I hope not too, John, because my books tell me that they lived and died by the dagger."

"Now that I think about it," William said, "I do remember hearing that they are very revengeful people and never forgive anyone who insults them."

"I read that too. A young Caucasian Prince, who was only twelve years old, boasted, 'I am at my eleventh head'."

"I don't believe it," the Duke exclaimed.

"It was also reported that he spoke French with a Parisian accent and coveted his father's bag of twenty-four rebel heads!"

"Now you are beginning to frighten me," William came in, "and if you do, I will simply stay on the yacht and refuse to set foot on the ground!"

"I cannot believe that they are as violent as they were when the book was written," Alnina commented, "but there is a vivid description here of the Battle in 1795 when Agha Mohammed, the Persian eunuch, took over Tiflis."

"What happened?" the Duke asked.

"His troops raped all the women they fancied and, as a memento of their victory, they hamstrung the right leg of every virgin taken."

"I have never heard of anything quite so appalling," William said. "I have a good mind to demand that you turn around here and now, John, and go back to nice old comfortable and safe England."

"It all happened a long time ago," Alnina said, "and I ought not to frighten you with it. But I must add that the women also knew how to fight and beneath their veils they often wore a dagger."

"I certainly don't blame them with that lot about!" William exclaimed.

"They were actually very brave. When they were besieged by the Russian Army in 1837, the women fought beside the men. When their ammunition was spent, they then flung rocks down on the attacking troops and, when there were no more rocks, the men hurled themselves to their deaths."

The Duke was listening intently and, looking at him with questioning eyes, Alnina finished,

"When the men were gone, the women flung down their children as missiles and leapt after them."

"I had no idea when William and I were there that all this had happened," the Duke remarked.

"It was all a long time ago," Alnina replied. "But it is interesting to know how brave the Tiflian women were and how much they valued their freedom. And they have always been very ferocious people."

The Duke then asked her,

"Well, you must tell us the rest, you have made my flesh creep as it is!"

Alnina smiled.

"One Chieftain found his son dead. He then cut his body into small pieces and sent his horsemen across the mountains, each one with a fragment to be given to his kinsmen."

"What happened then?" William enquired.

"For each piece an enemy's head was returned to him and his son's death was avenged."

"I only hope they have quietened down by now," the Duke said, "or we will never get home!"

"Of course they have," Alnina told him soothingly. "At the same time I still think they were very brave."

"Let's hope that the future will be less violent, but I am glad I have brought my revolver with me."

"That is slight comfort, John," William added, "but I can readily assure you, unless my friend who told me about Prince Vladimir was lying, an English Nobleman is more valuable to him than a Prince from another country."

"Then let's hope he looks after us and makes us comfortable while we are bargaining with him," the Duke murmured. "Perhaps if he values us as much as that, he might reduce the price or even give me the mountain as a present!"

William laughed.

"Only if you marry his daughter and that you have made certain you cannot do."

"Certainly not while I am there at any rate!" Alnina exclaimed. "I am sorry to have frightened you, but I think it's very interesting to know how brave the Georgians have been in the past."

They then talked about other matters.

When they finally went to bed, she thought that she had never enjoyed herself more.

It was fascinating to be able to talk with two such intelligent men and to discuss many subjects when recently she had had no one to talk to except Brooks and his wife.

She said a special prayer of thankfulness when she climbed to bed in the very comfortable cabin she had been allocated.

The Duke had, of course, taken the Master cabin, but she realised that hers was the best of the others.

It was decorated more prettily than even the Master cabin and it never struck her, although it had the Duke, that her cabin was the one always used by the Marquis's most favoured beauty.

He was noted for his *affaires de coeur* with a large number of the most acclaimed ladies in Society.

He was able to enjoy himself because his wife had been crippled after a fall out hunting and was obliged to live in the country. And, because she was having special treatment from the local doctor, she did not accompany her husband when he went to sea.

Alnina had led a very sheltered life, first at school and then with her father and therefore it did not strike her that her cabin was especially feminine.

"The curtains are such a lovely shade of pink," she said at dinner when they were talking about the yacht, "and I love the number of mirrors in my cabin, while the others have to be content with one or two at the most."

She did not notice the twinkle in the Duke's eye as he commented,

"It is a perfect beginning for anyone as beautiful as you. I feel the owner of this yacht must have been thinking of you when he decorated it!"

"As I have never met him, that is an easy thing to say," Alnina replied. "I am very happy to be in such a lovely cabin on such an exciting journey."

"I will drink to that," William came in, "but I don't want it to be too exciting. I have been thinking of what you told us at luncheon and I am only hoping that we will not have to use John's revolver to protect ourselves."

"I think we are safe for a while," the Duke replied. "At the same time I cannot be sure, if the Russians go on infiltrating into Asia as they are doing at the moment."

*

The next day, when breakfast was over, the Duke said that they should start their lessons, but Alnina must forgive him, he added, if he became so bored that he went away in the middle of them.

"I will try not to bore you," Alnina answered him. "But you will be far more bored when we reach Tiflis and

78

William and I chatter away with everyone we meet while you have to remain silent."

"Now you are bullying me," the Duke complained. "All right, I will try to speak the abominable language, but I will be extremely hostile if I fail!"

William laughed and teased him.

But they sat down in the Saloon and Alnina began their lesson.

She realised that it would definitely be a mistake for the Duke to be bored, so she concentrated on teaching them as quickly as possible the way a sentence was formed in Russian.

Then she told them very simple children's stories, which they had to translate from English into Russian.

They looked up the words they would require in a dictionary. It was the way Alnina herself had learnt herself which she had found amusing.

She was sure that was what the men would want, rather than just listening to what she said.

At the end of two hours they had certainly made no complaint. They merely thanked her and the Duke then went on deck for some fresh air.

It was what Alnina enjoyed herself for the rest of the afternoon, watching the waves breaking against the bow of the yacht.

When they reached the Bay of Biscay, she was so delighted to find that she was a good sailor, although at one time the sea was very rough.

At dinner the two men drank champagne and vied with each other in telling elaborate stories of ships at sea.

They tried to make Alnina's flesh creep and told her how in a storm a ship could be shattered on the rocks however strong it appeared to be.

"I refuse to let you scare me," she insisted. "It has been a long and interesting day and I am going to bed.

She smiled at both of them and added,

"Thank you, thank you so much for bringing me on this thrilling cruise. Whatever happens in the future, I will always remember it."

She walked towards the door as she spoke and, when she reached it, she turned and blew a kiss, first to William and then to the Duke.

"Good night and do sleep well," she said, "and be ready for lesson number two in the morning!"

When she had gone, the Duke poured himself out another drink.

"She is certainly a find," he said. "We might have searched England from top to toe without finding anyone so intelligent or indeed so beautiful."

"You will certainly be complimented on your wife if nothing else," William remarked. "Equally be careful, because that Prince is undoubtedly a nosy-parker. If he suspects for one moment you are deceiving him, I hate to think what your punishment would be."

"So do I," the Duke agreed. "After what Alnina told us about the Tiflians, I am really quite nervous about going there."

"I expect that they have settled down and are now enjoying peace and plenty instead of killing each other."

"That is true, but we fight when we have to," the Duke replied. "I am only afraid that, if the Russians go on behaving as they are at the moment in Bulgaria, we will find ourselves at war with them."

William did not reply.

Then the Duke remembered that his father had been a soldier and his mother had suffered acutely because of her fear that he might be killed. He had fought in many campaigns in obscure parts of the world, which made the British Empire greater than ever.

'I have never had a wish to fight anyone,' the Duke thought before he went to sleep. 'So I have been luckier than most men and I am extremely grateful for it.'

He was thinking of the huge house he had inherited with the title and the vast acres of land surrounding it.

There was also the large house in Berkeley Square, besides enough money for him to hire this yacht without for one moment having to consider the cost of it.

'How could I possibly have been so lucky?' he asked himself. I am extremely grateful to Fate which has been so kind to me.'

Then, when he did not want to think about her, he remembered the girl he had been in love from and who had jilted him three days before their wedding to marry a Viscount.

He had hated her and he had also despised himself for having believed that she loved him for himself.

Now unexpectedly he found it no longer hurt him as it had before to think about her and he could possibly understand why she had jilted him.

Just as he had longed to have that special mountain that he believed contained gold, so she had longed to wear a coronet at the Opening of Parliament and she had wanted to be acclaimed as someone of social importance because her husband was titled.

'I suppose really we all have a winning post in our minds which we want to reach,' the Duke thought. 'Now I have passed mine, I can be generous and no longer bitter.'

He gave a heartfelt sigh of satisfaction before he continued to think,

'I have been lucky, very very lucky.'

He stretched himself out in the big bed and then, instead of falling asleep as he intended, he began thinking of what he would do when he returned home.

Of course he still wanted to travel, but there was so much to be done in England. He thought that perhaps this particular journey would be his last for some time.

He was thinking new and unaccustomed thoughts when he fell asleep.

In the cabin next door Alnina was also thinking how happy she was and how lucky.

Who would have guessed for a moment when she was sitting alone at The Hermitage that a Duke would appear? It was almost as if he had dropped down from Heaven.

Before she really knew it was happening, she was here in this luxurious yacht and sailing towards one of the countries she had longed to visit, but thought she would never get further than illustrations of it in a book.

'I only hope,' she mused, 'that we don't arrive there too quickly or leave it the moment we arrive.'

She had read so much about Georgia and especially on the beauty of the Caucasus mountains and she felt as if she had already seen them, as if she had seen the glowing lowlands and beyond them the shadow of the mountains.

She had read in books that there was an atmosphere in Georgia of seduction, voluptuous adventures and even political uprising.

She wondered if she would really experience any of this.

She had also read of the vineyards and the orange groves and bazaars piled with silks and spices.

Persian jewellers were there weighting turquoises by the pounds and Caucasian armourers were working on beautiful damascened swords for which they were justly celebrated.

Her thoughts aroused in her a strange sensation that seemed to make her whole body glow.

'How could I be so fortunate,' she asked herself, 'as to be on my way to see a place such as that?'

She knew that ever since she had read about it, it had remained in her mind. It made her long for the East and yet she never thought that she would ever go there.

She said a little prayer of thanks.

Then she thought how difficult it was to thank the Duke enough for what he had already done for her.

She had known when she left The Hermitage that there was now no need to worry about it and both Brooks and Mrs. Brooks would have enough to eat and they were actually receiving their wages.

'They have been so kind to me,' she reflected, 'and I must take them back marvellous presents.'

Then she remembered that she did not have any money of her own.

The clothes she was wearing had been paid for by the Duke. The mere idea of it would have shocked her mother and all her older relations.

But they were not given to her as a gift – rather for the ulterior purpose of deceiving Prince Vladimir.

'I am sure it makes a difference,' she told herself.

At the same time she hoped that no one would ever know that the beautiful dresses she had bought in Bond Street had been paid for by a man!

'I have broken all the rules,' she thought. 'But not in the way other women would break them, immorally or just to enhance their own beauty.'

She then added to herself,

'I am doing it so that the Duke can achieve what matters to him, apparently much more than anything else – a mountain!'

It sounded so ridiculous that she had to laugh.

What other man could, she now asked herself, be so much in love with a mountain that he just had to own it, whatever the cost?

But then what other man would have taken her, disguised as his wife, on this exciting voyage?

'It's all unbelievable and that is what makes it so thrilling,' she told herself. 'I will always remember this journey when the Duke has no further use for me and I am sent home.'

She only hoped that things would not be as bad when she returned as when she left.

There were still some items left to sell and she had told the Solicitor exactly what she required for the different pieces she had pointed out to him.

He had argued with her over one inlaid table.

"I think that you should ask more than that, Miss Lester," he said. "That's a very fine table."

"But some of the mother-of-pearl inlay is missing," Alnina had said. "And I think it is only fair to point out to any purchaser that it will have to be restored."

"That can easily be done," the Solicitor had replied. "It's merely a question of money."

"Exactly," Alnina said, "and, as I have none, I shall be grateful to sell it even if it does not go for the top price it would have fetched had it been perfect."

"I will see what I can do," the Solicitor had said.

She knew by the way he spoke and the expression on his face that he was really determined to obtain what he considered the right sum for the table.

There were other pieces of furniture also which she was sure that he thought she was not asking as much for as they were worth.

At the same time it was impossible to tell him the truth – that she had been desperate for lack of enough money to pay for bread and butter!

'I am so lucky, so incredibly lucky,' Alnina said to herself, 'and it's all due to the Duke.'

She then snuggled down against the lace-trimmed pillow and as she did so she was thinking of him.

Suddenly she felt that strange little quiver within herself that she had felt when she looked into his eyes.

'He is wonderful,' she thought, 'so wonderful that I am half afraid he will suddenly disappear and I will never see him again.'

Then she laughed at herself.

She was making the Duke into a supernatural figure instead of what he was – just a man.

'But a very exceptional one,' she murmured as she turned over in bed.

Then she was too nervous of her own feelings to investigate them any further.

CHAPTER FIVE

The yacht steamed down the Mediterranean.

As it did so, the Duke was thinking that he had never known anyone as excited and enthusiastic as Alnina.

She was so thrilled with everything she saw and everything that he and William told her.

She was so pleased by the monkeys at Gibraltar that the Duke quite expected to be asked to take some with him.

Then, when they reached Italy, she longed to go to Rome, the Duke told her that he was in too much of a hurry and she would have to be content with Naples where they refuelled.

Naples, of course, was near Pompeii and Alnina had marvellous stories to tell them of what she had read on the eruption of Mount Vesuvius and the terrible destruction it caused in AD 79.

In fact the Duke told her that she was a walking encyclopaedia.

"I think that sounds very depressing," she replied. "Am I talking too much? Would you rather I was silent?"

"No of course not!" William piped up. "We are enjoying every moment of it! I only wish I knew as many stories about all these places as you do."

"I have read endlessly all about Europe," Alnina replied, "and I will be even more enchanted when we see the Greek Islands."

They teased her about the Greek Gods, saying they were who she really worshipped and she had to admit that she had a soft spot in her heart for Apollo.

"I so love everything about Greece," she enthused, "and perhaps one day I will be able to go there."

"Now you are making me feel guilty because we are not stopping at Athens," the Duke muttered.

"Perhaps, just perhaps," she sighed, "if we are not in a great hurry, we could stop there on our way back."

"I am making no promises, Alnina. You know as well as I do that you will want to stop everywhere and that would make us take three years to reach England! And by that time your house may have fallen down and they might have put another Duke in my place!"

Alnina laughed.

"I think that is unlikely because you are exactly what a Duke should be and your family must be grateful."

"I doubt if they are. To tell the truth I have paid them very little attention since I succeeded to the title."

"But of course they feel secure and happy because you are at the Head of the Family and that is exactly what a Duke is meant to do."

"Now I am interested, as you are talking about me. Now tell me if you think I am a perfect Duke or rather a disappointing one."

"You know the answer to that one already," Alnina said, "and you will become conceited if William and I keep paying you compliments."

She smiled before she went on,

"But of course we want you to be perfect and we want people to say you behave exactly as a Duke should behave! And I am sure they will."

"I often remember," William came in, "how John and I used to criticise the previous Head of the Family! We deplored him for keeping so much money for himself, instead of distributing it among us all."

"I expect that is what I will do too," the Duke said. "But for the moment, because it is so unusual to have any money at all, I enjoy giving it away."

"As you have given it to me," Alnina said softly.

"You are doing me a great service and I can hardly say that about any of my relations. In fact some of them are rather like your brother and seem to look on me as an ever open bank!"

"Well, doubtless you will be firm with them sooner or later," William said. "In the meantime I can assure you that they will criticise you heavily for wasting your money on buying a mountain."

"Whatever they think or do not think, I have every intention of having my precious mountain that I have loved for years. In fact I want to kiss her as soon as I arrive."

William held up his hand.

"Now the mountain has become a she!" he cried, "it's the last thing I expected. I have always been brought up to believe that mountains are men, whereas flowers are women!"

The Duke was firm in saying that as far as he was concerned his mountain was a female, even though, if he was asked, he preferred the male sex.

"Why should you prefer them?" Alnina asked.

"Because they are straightforward and honest, like myself, and don't cheat, as women invariably do sooner or later."

This sparked a long argument with Alnina speaking up for her own sex, while William refused to take sides.

"I will judge the issue," he volunteered, "and I will tell you at the end of the battle who is the winner."

It all ended by William declaring that there was no winner, but a draw between John and Alnina.

"Now we will go back to what I originally said when I told you my feeling for my mountain is that for a beautiful woman," the Duke said, having the last word.

"She is to me," he went on, "like Aphrodite or any of the other Greek Goddesses, compelling my admiration yet being out of reach and untouchable."

"You will have to touch the mountain whether you like it or not," William chuckled, "if we are to find the gold we think is in it."

"If she is as perfect as I imagine her to be and also as charming," the Duke replied, "I am sure the gold will pour out for us and we will not have half as much trouble in finding it as we thought."

William laughed and turned to Alnina,

"Let him dream his dreams. When he wakes up to reality, he will undoubtedly cry on our shoulders!"

"I think it is wonderful of him to have ideas which other people don't have," Alnina said, "and to have taken all this trouble to find his way back to his mountain."

"Wait until you see it. Then you will realise why I am so much in love with it."

The Duke then walked out of the Saloon and Alnina guessed that he was going up to the bridge.

"I think he believes that the ship goes faster when he is there," she confided to William.

"Between ourselves," William replied, "I am very worried in case when he gets there the mountain has blown up or, as I really suspect, the Prince will refuse to sell it."

"It is quite extraordinary that anyone as clever and practical as John," Alnina remarked, "should be such an idealist. In fact I am very impressed by him."

"So am I, but he has always been the same ever since we were at school together."

He paused as if he was looking back into the past.

"He used to make up his mind on something," he went on, "and invariably, because he was so determined, it came true."

"Then I hope he will not be disappointed now."

"I feel the same," William replied, "but between ourselves I think this time it's a hundred to one chance of realising his dreams."

"Oh, you must not say that! He will be terribly disappointed and we want him to be happy."

William grinned.

"I have never seen him as happy as he is at this moment. So we must just pray that the whole plot will not be a complete delusion."

"I already pray for that every night," Alnina said. "And I am hoping that everything will work out right and the Prince will let him have the mountain at a good price."

"Well, as far as I am concerned," William said, "I have enjoyed this voyage more than anything I have ever enjoyed before – and it is entirely due to you."

Alnina smiled at him.

"You are coming along really beautifully with your Russian," she said, "but John is so impatient with himself which is a mistake when it comes to learning languages."

"Well, at least we can now thank people politely and if we are stranded on a remote island where everyone speaks Russian, we can at least ask for something to eat."

"That is true and actually you have both been very quick in picking up what is a most difficult language."

"I only hope I don't have to converse with people at dinner or make a speech. Otherwise I think I will be able to cope with day to day affairs."

"I deliberately taught you that part first," Alnina said "because it is essential to be able to get yourself from place to place or buy food. The more conversational words can wait, but the ones I have just mentioned cannot."

"You have been wonderful, Alnina. I have never met a better teacher. If, as I said, we are stranded on a remote island, at least we will not starve."

When they came within sight of the Greek Islands, Alnina was permanently on deck running from one side of the yacht to the other so that she should not miss anything.

They anchored at night in quiet bays and every day seemed to Alnina to be more and more electrifying.

When finally they were about to leave the Sea of Marmara, she held her breath in case something should go wrong and they would not reach their destination, which the Duke had told her was the far end of the Black Sea.

She could not help feeling a little wistful as they were passing Constantinople, as she had always wanted to see that City which she had read so much about.

She had always been interested in the Sultans who succeeded each other and their harems grew bigger and bigger as each new Sultan tried to outdo the last one.

But she knew that it was useless to ask the Duke if he would stop even for a short visit to the City.

She therefore contented herself with viewing what she could with a pair of the Captain's binoculars.

Then at last they passed through the Bosporus and into the Black Sea.

Now the Duke was talking excitedly of what would happen when they arrived.

He had of course written to Prince Vladimir to say that he was coming and he also said that he was bringing with him his wife and a great friend, William Armstrong.

He wrote,

"*I am greatly looking forward to seeing Your Royal Highness again and I remember so well how beautiful the mountains looked when I last saw them from the Palace.*"

When he read the letter to William, he commented,

"You had better end up telling him he is wonderful or you will find that he will somehow manage to prevent you having what you are determined to acquire."

"Don't even think about it," the Duke stipulated. "I must have my own way. Heaven knows how much we have exerted ourselves to get to Georgia and they should in fact greet us with fireworks!"

"Heaven forbid," William had countered, "and just don't forget that, as Alnina is your wife, then she must be treated like a Duchess."

"You can be quite certain I will not forget that," the Duke had replied.

*

Having crossed the Black Sea, they spent the night on board at Batum and then they set off early the next morning for Tiflis.

Now, Alnina thought, they were really in Georgia and it would be just as attractive as had dreamed.

She had spent a lot of time during the last two days talking about the beauties they were going to behold.

"The two things" she said, "which really matter in Tiflis are, I am told, the excellent wines and the ancient Churches."

"I am certainly interested in the first," William said.

In the morning at the Port they found a carriage drawn by four strong horses waiting for them.

There was also another vehicle, not so impressive, to carry their luggage and Albert.

When Alnina saw the countryside for the first time, it was exactly as beautiful, at the same time as mysterious, as she had anticipated.

She was utterly enthralled by the distant hills and the first glimpse of the mountains and the fortified villages still seemed prepared for war at any time.

It was impossible, she thought, to see it now so peaceful and so quiet without thinking how it had been the scene of more bloodshed and more cruelty and hatred than any other country in that part of the world.

Everywhere in Georgia, she had learnt, there were extremes.

Tigers roamed the tropical Eastern lowlands, while eagles soared above the gaunt uplands.

Gigantic mountains straddled the land, the White Mountains, the Black Mountains, the many ravines. She had read about the mountains, where the bats fly both day and night, because some valleys never see the sun and are cloaked in gloom.

Now she could see it for herself she found that it was all fascinating.

So much so that she did not speak and the Duke turned to ask her why she was so quiet.

"There are no words to express what I am feeling," she replied. "I only wish I could write a poem or a song to describe what we are seeing on either side of us."

"I expect we will have plenty of songs when we reach Tiflis. As far as I remember, there was always noise in the streets and endless music in the Palace."

It took them just seven hours, including a short stop for lunch, to reach Tiflis.

As Alnina had expected, it was a very attractive little City in what was described in books as the 'glowing lowlands'.

Now at last she could have the first glimpse of the towering mountains.

She felt a thrill run through her and was almost sure that the Duke was feeling the same.

The Palace, when they drew up outside it, was not as large as she had expected, but at the same time it was extremely attractive with a mass of flowers and blossoming trees surrounding it and there were fountains playing on either side of the drive up to the front door.

"Now we must all be on our best behaviour," the Duke said. "Don't forget that he thinks himself extremely important, and you, Alnina, must curtsey low to him."

"I would do so anyway because he is the Ruler over the most beautiful country I have ever seen," she replied.

"Wait until you see the mountains. Then you will really draw in your breath."

She knew by the note of excitement in the Duke's voice that was how he was feeling and she thought it very touching that the mountains mattered so much to him.

They were greeted at the front door by a number of strangely dressed attendants as they entered the Palace.

They were then taken immediately to where they were told that His Royal Highness was waiting for them.

The Duke remembered just in time to offer Alnina his arm and then they entered the Prince's private room as if they were a married couple.

The Prince was very much as she expected.

A tall good-looking man with the strong features that all Georgians boasted. His eyes had a sharpness about them and it was as if he was searching inside the person he talked to, rather than listening to what they were saying.

The Prince rose as they entered the room and held out his hand to the Duke.

"My dear Duke," he said in French. "I am very delighted to see you. I hope you had a good journey here."

"We did it in almost record time," the Duke replied. "It is a great pleasure and we are very honoured by Your Royal Highness's kind invitation to stay with you."

"I am so pleased that you are my guests," the Prince replied graciously.

"Now I would like to present my wife," the Duke asked, "whom you have not yet met and my friend William Armstrong whom you met on my last visit?"

"I remember Mr. Armstrong," the Prince said, "and of course I am delighted to meet Madame la Duchesse."

Alnina swept to the ground in a low curtsey and it was quite obvious that the Prince approved.

They sat down at the Prince's invitation and were given tea in small cups without handles and there was also delicious French *pâté* that Alnina thought could only have been made by a French chef.

Then the Prince said,

"I am most anxious for you to meet my daughter, Natasha. She is now seventeen and I hope will soon be married."

"Is she engaged?" the Duke enquired.

"No, no!" the Prince replied quickly, "but I am very anxious that she should marry an Englishman. I have in fact, been in correspondence with the British Embassy."

"I am sure they were most helpful," the Duke said. "And I am certain that you will find a number of delightful Englishmen who will be only too pleased to marry Your Royal Highness's daughter."

There was silence for a moment and Alnina knew that the Prince was thinking that the Duke would have been an excellent choice.

Almost as if he read her thoughts, the Prince said,

"I am very surprised to learn that you have become the Duke of Burlingford. When you were last here, you did not tell me that the title was waiting for you."

"It was not waiting for me when I was last here," the Duke replied. "In fact it was a great surprise when both my relative and his unmarried son were drowned at sea."

"So that was how you came into the title!"

"Exactly and, of course, it is a great responsibility I never expected to have. At the same time I am fortunate in having the help of my wife, who comes from an ancient and distinguished family."

"And have you known her a long time?"

"Both William and I were at the same school as her brother, Lord Lester," the Duke answered.

He was about to say that her brother was dead, then thought it would be a mistake. He therefore went on,

"If you want your daughter to marry an Englishman then I think you should take her to England. If you stay with friends, they will undoubtedly introduce you to all the most charming gentlemen who are, as you can imagine, pursued by *debutantes* and *jeunes filles* hoping for a title."

Again he was thinking of his own engagement and there was a slightly sarcastic note in his voice.

They talked for a little while and then the Prince suggested,

"I must allow you to rest, as I am giving a special party for you tonight with dancing to a new band which has recently arrived from Paris."

"It sounds delightful," the Duke said. "I am sure my wife, who speaks French fluently, will enjoy meeting any of your French friends who may be among the guests and, of course, I am certain that most of your own people also speak French."

"The French Ambassador will be present tonight," he answered, "and a number of visitors who come here from Paris because they find Georgia so attractive."

An equerry showed them up to their rooms, which were in another part of the Palace away from the Prince's private rooms.

Alnina found that she and the Duke had been given a large bedroom overlooking the garden.

For a moment she thought with alarm that there was only one room and one bed.

Then the Duke found another door leading out to a dressing room for him and to Alnina's relief she saw that it also contained a single but comfortable-looking bed.

"So far, so good," the Duke said to her in English, but the equerry had already disappeared.

"I think the Prince is rather frightening," Alnina said, "but I am looking forward to seeing his daughter."

"It's a pity William does not have a title," the Duke murmured.

"I don't think William would like to live here for ever and he told me he has only a small house in England which would not be very suitable for a Princess."

"You are now saving me from being ambushed," the Duke said, "and you know I am very grateful."

She smiled at him and then went back to her room, where a maid was busy unpacking her clothes.

As there was to be a party that night, Alnina chose the most glamorous dress she had bought in Bond Street.

The Duke had also given her before they left a large jewel case filled with jewels that had been passed down century after century by his ancestors.

"The one thing that always impresses foreigners," he said, "is jewellery. But for Heaven's sake don't lose them or the family will have hysterics."

"I only hope we can lock them up in a safe."

"It's easier to lock the case and you can sleep on it at night and carry it with you all day!"

The Duke was teasing her, but for a moment she thought he was serious and then she laughed.

"If it is to be carried all day," she said, "then any polite gentleman would, of course, carry it for his wife or any lady who was with him."

"All right," the Duke conceded, "you win, but as I just said, for Heaven's sake don't lose the family jewels."

"I will do my best to preserve them, but I am sure that you are making the Prince most upset because you are not eligible as a potential son-in-law."

"When I see his daughter," the Duke replied, "I am sure that I will be glad I have had a lucky escape."

Actually, when they went down to dinner and met with Princess Natasha, she was far more attractive than the Duke had anticipated.

In fact, Alnina thought, she was very pretty indeed.

She was dark and very Russian-looking and at the same time she had a sweet smile and was quite obviously thrilled to meet people from other countries.

"You must tell me about England," she said to Alnina soon after they had been introduced. "My father is always talking about it, but I don't see how I can get there unless I fly like a bird."

Alnina laughed.

"You must make your father take you to England in a ship," she said. "It has been a marvellous voyage for us in the Duke's yacht and I have enjoyed every second of it."

She realised after she had spoken that she should have referred to him as her husband and not as the Duke and she hoped it was a slip the Princess did not notice.

William was now making himself charming to her.

Dinner was a delicious meal, cooked clearly by a French chef.

The guests were nearly all French and even if they were Georgian they spoke French with the Prince.

When the music started for them to dance after dinner, the Prince asked Alnina for the first dance.

She found to her surprise he danced extremely well.

"I hope you are enjoying yourself, *madame*," he said.

"I am enjoying every moment," Alnina replied. "I am thrilled to find that Georgia is just as beautiful as it was described in the books I have read about it."

"I love my country, therefore I am so pleased when beautiful women, like yourself, praise it."

"I will praise it even more when I have seen the Caucasus Mountains," Alnina said, "and at even a brief glimpse I found them enthralling."

"I hope you will find them as beautiful as I find you," the Prince replied.

She smiled at the Prince. It was just the sort of compliment she felt a Frenchman would pay her and it was hard to think that he had not stepped out directly from the *Rue de la Paix*.

"Now tell me," he was saying, "how I can find an English husband for my little daughter, Natasha."

"She is so pretty that I don't think there will be any difficulties about it."

"And you will help me to find the right man?" the Prince asked.

Alnina, of course, said she would be delighted to do so, but at the same time she thought that they were skating on rather thin ice.

If the Prince bought her to England, he would learn that the Duke was not married.

It would be revealed that he was a liar and she was an imposter.

"I wonder," she said rather tentatively, "why you don't choose a French husband for your daughter. After all, you all speak perfect French here and I think on the whole a Frenchman is more adapted to other countries than an Englishman is."

"France is not as important in the world as England is," he replied. "Thus I am determined that my daughter will have an English husband."

As he spoke, he glanced towards the Duke, who was dancing with Princess Natasha.

Alnina thought that there was almost an unpleasant look in his eyes.

It was as if he blamed the Duke for not telling him on his first visit that he was likely to come into a title.

So in order to change the subject, she talked again about Georgia and the Caucasus Mountains.

They were still talking when they left the ballroom to sit outside in the garden.

Nothing, Alnina thought, could be more beautiful.

The moon was creeping slowly up the sky to join the stars and, with the scent of flowers all round them and music coming through the open windows, it all seemed too exquisite to be real.

"And I am enchanted, absolutely enchanted by your country and your Palace," Alnina told him.

"I hope perhaps you will add its owner to your list."

Alnina smiled.

"My husband told me how charming you were and I have been looking forward to meeting you."

"And now we have met, are you disappointed?"

"No, of course not. You fit so perfectly with this beautiful background and undoubtedly play the lead in this delightful drama."

Alnina was choosing her words carefully. But she thought as she spoke that they sounded too romantic.

To her surprise the Prince took her hand and raised it to his lips and for a moment she thought it a strange thing for a Georgian to do.

Then she remembered that everything they did, like the way they spoke, was French and it was just how a Frenchman would have behaved.

She and the Prince went back to the ballroom to find that Princess Natasha was still dancing with William.

The Duke was looking for her and, as he walked towards her, she felt the Prince straighten himself.

Once again she was aware that he was looking at the Duke in a somewhat unpleasant manner. It was not only what she could see, but what she could feel.

She felt certain, although he had never said a word against the Duke, that he actually disliked him.

Later that night when they went up to bed, the Duke walked with Alnina into her bedroom in case anyone was watching them.

"Have you enjoyed yourself tonight?" he asked.

"I have enjoyed it all immensely," Alnina replied. "but I do think we have to be rather careful of the Prince."

"Why?" the Duke questioned.

"I don't know why," Alnina replied, "but I feel he dislikes you."

"Nonsense! He was always most friendly when I was here before. I am sure now he is doing his very best to welcome us."

"I may be imagining things, but although he danced with me several times and did not seem to be interested in dancing with anyone else, I had the distinct feeling that he was watching you."

"I think you are exaggerating, Alnina. Of course he may be somewhat annoyed that I have come into a title when he might have pushed his daughter off onto me when I was here before and unmarried."

"I am sure that he would have done that if he had known you were to become a Duke," Alnina said. "He kept talking about how he wanted her to have an English husband and I replied that he must bring her to England. Then I realised that, if he did, he would learn that we are not married."

"Well, all I can say is that I am extremely grateful to you. If I had come here unmarried, I am sure I would have been forced somehow into marriage and as you well know, it is what I intend absolutely to avoid."

"I have certainly received that message loud and clear. John, and I consider it an insult to my sex that you prefer a mountain to any of us."

"Wait until you see it, Alnina, and then you will understand."

"Have you arranged to go there?" she asked.

"I certainly have and William and I will be leaving as soon as we have finished breakfast. I thought you could spend the morning exploring the little shops and the many bazaars in Tiflis. It's not very far to walk."

"Of course the mountain comes first – "

"You are laughing at me. Therefore the sooner I go to bed the better. Goodnight, Alnina, and may I say that you have played your part brilliantly tonight. No Duchess could have been more dignified or, may I say it, more attractive."

Alnina curtseyed to the Duke.

"Thank you, kind sir," she murmured.

He opened the communicating door, then paused.

"Goodnight again, Alnina. If you are disturbed or frightened in the night, you know I am next door."

"I hope, like the Georgians, you will have your revolver with you," Alnina replied.

"I think to be correct, it ought to be a dagger," the Duke said. "Actually the answer to that question is 'yes'."

"Then I really feel protected."

"I have locked your door for you and unless an intruder climbs through the window it is unlikely you will be disturbed."

"Thank you," Alnina said, "and thank you again for everything. It is all even more wonderful than I expected."

"That is exactly what I wanted to hear you say."

He left the room and closed the communicating door between them.

Alnina began to undress.

She could not help thinking it was all very strange and she felt all the time that they were acting on a stage rather than living in real life.

Of one thing she was quite certain.

If the Prince managed to find out that the Duke was not married, he would certainly make every possible effort to marry his daughter to him.

'She is a nice girl, but very Russian,' she thought, 'not only to look at but to hear her talking. I doubt if she would make the Duke happy.'

As she climbed into bed, she thought how thrilling everything was.

She had never expected to find herself in a Palace and how different it was from her own house where she was selling everything that was worth any money.

'I will be able to look back on this and feel quite sure that it was just my imagination,' she told herself.

Then, because it had been a very invigorating but tiring day, she fell asleep.

CHAPTER SIX

The next morning the Duke was determined to have a word with the Prince about the mountain he wanted to buy.

And then he had decided that he and William would visit it to make quite certain that the place where he had originally seen the gold had not subsequently been mined.

He had not said a word to anyone at the time, but he was sure that, if there had been further exploration and development, he would have heard about it in one way or another.

The Duke went to the Prince's private sitting room immediately after breakfast.

The Prince was waiting for him.

"I have been wanting a word with you, my dear Duke," he said, as soon as they had sat down, "about my daughter, Natasha."

"I have been thinking about her," the Duke said quickly. "My wife and I would suggest that you send her to London and I will find her a delightful and influential chaperone to stay with."

Before the Prince could answer one way or another, the Duke went on,

"Now I have something to ask of you. When I was here last, I was very taken with the mountain right at the end of the Caucasus range. It is, of course, on your land. I have had an ambition ever since to own a mountain and I would very much like to buy that one from you."

The Prince looked at him in surprise.

"You want to buy it!" he exclaimed.

The Duke nodded.

"I suppose every man dreams of owning something unique and different and I want you to make my dream come true."

"You *really* want my mountain?"

It was as if he could not believe what he had heard.

"I just want a mountain that is mine," the Duke said firmly. "No mountain I have ever seen is quite as beautiful and striking as that one."

There was silence and then the Duke added,

"It would make me exceedingly happy to own it."

"It is something I must think about seriously," the Prince said. "The mountain has belonged to the Palace and my family for many centuries and it might upset our people to let someone who is a foreigner become the owner of it."

"I see your difficulty, but I am prepared to pay a good price for it and, of course, as I can hardly take it away with me, you will have the pleasure of looking at it in the future just as you do today."

He thought the Prince would feel assured by that statement, but he merely answered,

"I must think about it. I must consider your idea very seriously!"

"Of course you must," the Duke said. "Meanwhile I would like to take William and look more closely at the mountain than I was able to do when I was last here."

"I can understand that," the Prince remarked, "and I will tell my overseer to take you there and show you the best way into the large cavern, which I think you found when you were here before."

"I want to go inside and explore it again and, when I come back, I will make you a very large offer for it."

The Duke smiled before he continued,

"It will certainly pay for the beautiful gowns your daughter will require when she takes London by storm."

The Prince smiled and replied,

"I was expecting that to be expensive!"

"It will be, but she will look very lovely and will doubtless enchant a great number of distinguished young gentlemen."

He thought that the Prince was pleased at the idea.

Then, as he was in a hurry to see the mountain, he left the Prince and went to find William, also the overseer who was to escort them there.

As soon as they had left, the Prince went to find Alnina.

She had been told by the Duke what he was going to do and so, having finished breakfast, she had gone into the garden.

She would have liked to go with him, but he had not invited her and she knew instinctively that he wanted to go alone with William as he had before. They wanted to make certain that there had been no development in the large cavern and that the gold was still actually there.

Alnina found herself a comfortable seat among the flowers.

She was thinking how beautiful they were when she saw the Prince standing outside the Palace.

He was looking round the garden and she hoped that he would not notice her, as she wanted to enjoy the serenity of the flowers alone.

But when the Prince saw where she was, he came walking towards her.

Alnina rose and curtseyed.

"I thought somehow that I would find you here," he said, "and that my flowers would attract you."

"They are lovely, perfectly lovely," Alnina replied. "I wish I could have a photograph of them."

"I never thought of having them photographed, but I will certainly have it done especially for you."

Alnina smiled at him.

"Thank you very much, as it will be something to remember when it is raining in England or very cold. Then there is nothing in the garden but weeds."

She made it sound very pitiful, spoken in French, and the Prince laughed.

Then he said,

"I think it would still be beautiful if you were there, *madame*."

"I enjoy your compliments, Your Royal Highness, and, as you well know, no one can pay them better than the French and that is why they always sound so right in that language."

"I would rather say them in Russian, but I feel you might not understand them."

Alnina was about to say that she spoke Russian and then she thought it would be a mistake. It was a language few women in England would ever learn and therefore he might think it odd that she could speak it and somehow connect it with her presence here with the Duke.

There was no doubt that the Prince was very acute.

She had realised last night when sitting beside him at dinner that he was very interested in English social life.

She suspected that he read the English newspapers whenever they were available and so he might suspect that

108

the Duke was not married, even though she had arrived here as his wife.

"What I am wondering now," he was saying while she was ruminating, "is would you be interested in coming with me to see the Caucasus Mountains?"

Alnina turned to him with a murmur of excitement.

"Not the one that your husband is interested in," he went on, "but a little further up where the mountains are staggeringly high above a vast ravine."

"Oh, do take me there," Alnina cried.

"I am sure you would find it not only beautiful," the Prince said, "but unique in that nowhere else in the world are there mountains like ours."

He spoke with a note of pride she did not miss and she was afraid that, if he felt like that, he would not want to sell his own mountain to anyone.

However it was an invitation she could not refuse and she said,

"Of course I would love to come with you and see the mountains. I was thinking about them all the time we were coming here."

"Then I will order a carriage," the Prince said, "and I expect that you will want to put on a hat."

"I would rather take a sunshade, but then you might be ashamed of me, driving out beside you without being properly dressed."

"You look breathtakingly lovely just as you are."

Again in French his compliment sounded far more sincere than it would have done in English.

Carrying her sunshade and with only a small bow of ribbon in the front of her long fair hair, Alnina climbed into the open carriage.

It was to take them through the town and up to the place where the Prince told her that the mountains were most beautiful.

As they drove off, the Prince began,

"This is a range that I think is the most exquisite of all the mountains and I have, as you can imagine, visited them hundreds of times since I was a little boy."

"This is very very exciting for me," Alnina replied. "I have read that the forests are particularly extensive on the Southern slopes of the Caucasus range."

"That is true, but first I would like you to see how charming our little town is. People come from all over Georgia to buy our jewellery and the embroidery made by our women."

Alnina did not say that she had read all about it in her books, but instead asked him questions and the answers she found more interesting than anything she had read.

She saw the vineyards as they passed them and the large orange groves and, when they came to the bazaar, the Prince ordered the driver to go very slowly.

Alnina could see the Persian jewellers with their jewels glittering in the sun.

She longed to stop and buy some silk garments, but the coachman had his orders and they moved out of the bazaar and into the countryside.

As the carriage drove on, the Prince pointed out the rooftops where in the evening the Georgian beauties took the air.

"They fan themselves," he told her, "and eye the swaggering warriors who prowl about in their soft leather boots."

"I am told they are very dangerous fighting men – "

"You only have to read our history to know that, by hook or by crook or rather by gun and dagger, we always get what we want."

He spoke in a way that sounded rather threatening and she quickly turned the conversation to other matters.

She watched the children, who looked well fed and were running beside the horses.

Then they were free of the town and now she could see the mountains rising higher and higher on one side of her, the trees closing in on the other.

They drove a long way before the Prince ordered the carriage to come to a standstill.

Then he helped Alnina out of the carriage and they walked on a narrow path above a deep ravine.

On the other side were mountains reaching up so high into the sky that Alnina felt she was in darkness.

Yet here there were trees and more trees and the sun caught the leaves and turned them to gold.

It was now that Alnina felt fully conscious of the entrancing atmosphere she had read so much about.

She was being drawn by it up onto the very top of the mountain and from there she would be able to see the whole world beneath her.

She stood gazing at it all and knew that she was completely enchanted by the majestic view.

She had no idea that the Prince was looking at her with a strange expression in his eyes.

Finally after what seemed like a century of time had passed, he led her back to the carriage.

She had one last look at the mountains and in the far distance she could see that the peaks were higher still with snow lingering on the very tops.

Then, as she sank back into the carriage, the Prince put his hand over hers.

"I know what you were feeling," he said. "It's what I felt myself when I first stood in that particular spot and saw the mountains soaring above me."

"You are very fortunate," Alnina replied, "to have anything so beautiful and so moving right here on your doorstep."

"And the Duke is extremely lucky to have you as his wife. Have you been married for long?"

"No, only a very short time. My husband has with him a photograph of our wedding and I know he is anxious to show it you."

The Prince did not speak and Alnina went on,

"This is our honeymoon, as, owing to mourning, our marriage had to be delayed."

She was saying the first thought that came into her head.

The Prince's hand was still on hers and he was now looking at her in a way that she felt was embarrassing.

"You are very beautiful," the Prince murmured.

Lifting her hand he kissed it.

As they were speaking in French and it was very much a French gesture, it was of no significance.

But still feeling rather uncomfortable she continued to talk about the Duke.

She was trying to impress the Prince by enthusing about his great estate in Scotland.

"He also has a charming house in London," she said, "which is very convenient when we want to visit my home which is only a short distance out into the country."

"And your mother and father?"

"They are dead and my brother died tragically in an accident."

"So you have no one to live in your family home?"

"That is indeed true. There is no one to take over the house."

"And you have no other brothers?" he enquired.

Alnina shook her head.

"No, and I have not yet discovered any relation to inherit it."

She thought as she spoke about the family treasures she had left behind which she hoped were being sold while she was away.

Because she looked worried, the Prince said,

"So what has upset you? What are you thinking about? Let me banish it from your mind so that you look happy again."

"I am happy," Alnina insisted, "very happy because I am here."

Remembering that she was supposed to be on her honeymoon, she added,

"I am only sad when I think about my brother and how much he would have enjoyed, as I have myself, your beautiful mountains."

"I want you to be happy," the Prince said. "When a woman is happy she looks much more alluring than at any other time."

Alnina smiled.

"Then, of course, I will try to look happy all the time I am with you and it's not very difficult for me when you have such beautiful surroundings to live in and above all your magical mountains."

"Now you are looking happy again."

113

To her surprise the Prince kissed her hand again.

They arrived back at the Palace to find that the Duke and William were already there.

They were, in fact, having a glass of champagne when Alnina and the Prince arrived.

Alnina walked towards the Duke and he then bent forward and kissed her on the cheek.

For a moment she was almost startled and then she realised that, as the Prince was standing just behind her, it was exactly what he should do.

"Have you enjoyed yourself," the Duke asked.

"It was wonderful, the most beautiful and exciting scenery I have ever experienced," Alnina replied.

She longed to ask him if he had felt the same, but the Duke was now saying to the Prince.

"Thank you for being so kind to my wife. I knew it was something that she must see before we left. But I too, have enjoyed my trip with William to the special mountain that belongs to you."

There was a meaning behind his words and the Prince replied,

"I am so glad that you have enjoyed yourself."

Then he walked away as if he had no wish to have a further conversation about the mountain.

*

Alnina had only just enough time to tidy herself before luncheon.

Quite a number of people had been invited to meet them. They all spoke French and there was no question of a Russian word being heard in the dining room.

When luncheon was over, they went out into the garden to admire the flowers.

By now the sun had grown so hot that Alnina was glad of her sunshade.

It was impossible to have a private word with the Duke and she was really longing to know what they had discovered while she had been away with the Prince.

William was deeply engaged in conversation with Princess Natasha and they were laughing together.

Alnina was sure that they had found nothing wrong, for if so, William would be looking depressed.

The people who had come to luncheon stayed for a long time and some of them, who had come from a long distance actually stayed for tea.

Being aristocrats they spoke French and behaved in the French manner and they had no wish for the tea which was supplied for Alnina and the Duke because they were English.

It was certainly not a very English-looking spread, but Alnina was glad of the tea in the cups without handles and the small pieces of *pâté* that went with it.

Yet it was a relief when tea was over and, as the guests disappeared, she then hurried upstairs to her room, feeling sure that the Duke would follow her.

Very soon he knocked on the door and came in.

"I thought we would never be able to be alone," Alnina said. "I am dying to know if you found things as you hoped they would be."

"The mountain seems to have been untouched since we last visited it," the Duke replied, "but William and I could not find the traces of gold we had seen on our last visit."

"Have they been removed?" Alnina asked.

The Duke shook his head.

"No, what seems to have occurred is that moss and other vegetation that grows thickly over the mountain have covered the places we had investigated."

"How amazing!" Alnina exclaimed.

"Although we said we preferred to be on our own," the Duke continued, "the overseer who had been ordered to take us to the mountain never left us."

"How infuriating. So you have no idea if the gold is still there."

"I think it must be although we could not find the traces of it that we did before. But we can always go back tomorrow and perhaps the day after and somehow contrive to be alone."

As he spoke, he took some small implements from the pocket of his coat.

He had intended to use them, but they were still clean and dry and it was quite obvious that he had not even taken them out of his pocket.

Alnina gazed at them thinking that they were very small.

Then the Duke explained,

"We have brought bigger and better tools here with us, but needless to say we could not have made use of them if in fact the Prince was informed, as he would have been, of what we were doing."

"I am very sorry for you," Alnina sighed. "As I enjoyed my expedition very much."

"I will indeed speak to the Prince again and perhaps tomorrow we can go there alone."

"I hope so for your sake. It must have been very upsetting for you, but I am sure you will win in the end."

The Duke smiled.

"You are always very consoling and you make me believe that everything finally will come right."

"Of course it will. It will be a tragedy if you don't possess the mountain you have loved so much for so long."

"I think really the luckiest thing that has happened was my finding you and you have undoubtedly been a huge success. The Prince would, I am sure, have married me off to his daughter if you had not been here."

"He is absolutely determined," Alnina said, "to find an English husband for her. But I cannot help feeling, as things are at the moment, it will not be easy."

"No, of course not. When Queen Victoria is furious with the Czar because of his behaviour in the Balkans, she is obviously not going to encourage an aristocrat to marry a Russian Princess."

There was silence for a while and then Alnina said,

"She is a very pretty girl and I can see that William finds her quite delightful. As this is Georgia and not really Russia, perhaps you made a mistake in avoiding marrying her?"

"If I married her, it would be the biggest mistake any man could make," the Duke replied seriously.

He spoke so positively that Alnina was silenced.

Then to change the subject she asked,

"When are you going to your mountain again?"

"Tomorrow morning and, if the Prince still insists on sending a nosy-parker like we had with us today, I think it might be wise if I suggested that you come with us."

"I think that the Prince will want to take me driving again. He did talk about another place where there was an even better view of the mountains than this morning's. But it is further away."

"Whatever that view is like, I still want to buy this mountain," the Duke persisted. "I will talk to him about it this evening if I get the opportunity. Keep him amused and keep him happy. Then maybe he will think it an attraction to have us on his estate."

As the Duke finished speaking, he walked into his own room.

Alnina wanted to query the word 'us', but thought it best not to do so.

She then started to undress, hoping a servant would bring her a bath before dinner.

There were more guests who arrived before Alnina went downstairs and the Duke had gone ahead of her.

She was wearing yet another beautiful gown that she had bought in Bond Street.

She received some delightful compliments from the visitors as well as one from the Prince.

Again she was sitting on his right at dinner and he said to her quietly as they sat down,

"You grow more ravishing every time I see you."

"And you become more magnificent," she replied, "when I think of your wonderful mountains and, of course, your exquisite garden."

The Prince laughed.

"You are very English, *madame*. Only the English think that their gardens are more important than anything else."

"Who told you that?" Alnina enquired.

"I think it was an English lady who came here last year and, like you, went into ecstasies over the garden. In fact, it impressed her even more than the mountains."

"That is why I am different. Your mountains come first for me and then your garden."

"And where do I come in?" the Prince asked.

"Where else could you possibly be, except on the top of everything? And that is where you must stay!"

She was thinking that in some way the Czar might dispose of him in the same way as he had disposed of the Balkan Principalities as the Russians took them over.

Then she realised that the Prince had taken it as a personal compliment.

She therefore added,

"No one could ask for more than to live in such an enchanted land, where I am sure that even the eagles wear coronets!"

The Prince laughed.

Glancing down the table she felt the Duke would be pleased that she was keeping him in such good humour.

'Surely as they are so friendly, he will let John have what he wants,' Alnina said to herself.

However she was not quite certain. Anything was possible in this strange and unpredictable world.

She could understand that the Duke and William were feeling frustrated.

After dinner they danced again.

Alnina learnt that the band belonged entirely to the Palace. It was available when the Prince desired music at any time of the day or night.

The new guests danced better than those who had been there the previous night.

Alnina found herself dancing with one man after another until the Prince protested,

"I do want to dance with you, but someone always snatches you away," he said. "Now I must insist on having my favourite waltz played and we will dance for a long time."

Alnina smiled at him.

"We must not be too tired for our new expedition tomorrow," she said. "I want you to show me a great deal more of your fantastic country."

"That is what I am anxious to do," the Prince said, "and by the way, today you did promise to show me all the photographs you have with you. I am very interested in photography which I know very little about and I would like more than anything else to have a photograph of you."

"Of course you will have one," Alnina said, "and we brought some taken at our wedding especially to show you."

That she thought was very true.

As she preferred telling the truth to acting a lie, she told the Prince the trouble William had in taking them.

"Professional photographers in the country are few and far between," she said. "But William brought his new camera down to my house and I am sure you will think that John and I looked very smart."

"I am sure you looked lovely," the Prince said.

Because she thought it would interest him, she told him about her special wedding dress.

"My father bought it in China for my mother," she said, "but it fitted me extremely well."

"You must not forget to give me a photograph of you in it," the Prince said.

"I promise I will give you one."

It was one o'clock in the morning before the guests finally said goodnight and the band retired.

"We all need our beauty sleep," the Duke declared.

But he and William drank a nightcap before they went upstairs.

The Prince had already said goodnight and gone to his own room.

The Duke said to William,

"We will be off early tomorrow morning and try to make sure that what was in the mountain is still there. We will also make it quite clear that we want to be alone."

He was speaking in a very low voice.

Yet Alnina was sure the equerry who was waiting for them to go to bed could not understand English, but she did not think he was as ignorant as he pretended to be.

"Come along," she said, "the sooner we go upstairs the better."

"I am only too willing," the Duke replied. "I am tired and I expect you are too."

"I have enjoyed dancing, as I have not danced for a long time."

"Very well, I will give a ball for you, Alnina, when we return to England," the Duke suggested.

"I only hope you will keep your promise," Alnina said. "You know that I would enjoy it more than anything else."

"And I say the same," William came in. "So don't worry. I will keep him up to scratch."

They walked upstairs and then William went to his room and Alnina and the Duke to theirs.

The Duke she thought seemed rather tired, but no less enthusiastic than he had been on the previous day.

When they entered the bedroom, he walked towards the communicating door.

"Goodnight, Alnina," he called out, "do sleep well. You have been splendid all day, absolutely splendid."

He did not wait for her reply, but went straight into the dressing room, shutting the door behind him.

It was then she saw lying on the table in front of the window the photographs which they had brought in a large envelope.

She had promised to show them to the Prince and she thought after his kindness to her today that it would be a nice gesture for her to give them to him before he went to bed.

If he had left his private room, she would put them where he could see them first thing tomorrow morning.

Picking up the envelope, she opened her door and went down the stairs.

There were no equerries in the hall and the lights were low, although it was easy to see the way.

She went down the passage that led to the Prince's private sitting room.

As she reached the door, she heard his voice inside and realised that he was not alone.

He was talking in Russian.

She hesitated, wondering if she should knock and give him the photographs or put them on the floor for him to find when he had finished his conversation.

Then she heard him say the Duke's name.

He pronounced it in a rather strange way so that it sounded somewhat different from how it did in English.

"Burlingford and his friend William Armstrong will be going to the mountain again tomorrow," he said.

"Why is he so interested in it?" asked the man he was talking to.

He was speaking in Russian as well.

But Alnina knew from his accent that he was not a very cultured man.

"I have no idea," the Prince then replied, "unless he believed it contains gold or precious stones."

The other man laughed.

"Your Royal Highness made absolutely sure about that many months ago and, if that's what the Englishman's seeking, he'll be disappointed."

"Not only disappointed," the Prince added. "Take him up onto that ledge which should not be difficult and, as many other people have done, he will slip over the edge."

"Your Royal Highness wishes to dispose of him?" the man asked.

"That is what I want," the Prince replied.

"And the man with him?"

"That is immaterial. He is of no consequence."

There was silence for a moment and then the Prince said, almost as if he was speaking to himself,

"Then Madame la Duchesse will be free and will become my wife!"

"That's very clever of Your Royal Highness," the man said, "and, as she's English, it'll be very acceptable to our people."

"I thought that was what you would think and feel," the Prince said, "and, as she is amazingly lovely we will doubtless have a son, perhaps several, to inherit."

"That's what all your people pray for, Your Royal Highness," the man replied.

Alnina drew in her breath.

Then she was afraid the conversation was coming to an end and they might find her outside the door.

On tiptoe she hurried back the way she had come and, as before, the hall was empty.

She ran up the stairs to her own room, feeling her heart beating tumultuously.

The envelope with the photographs was quivering in her hand as if blown by the wind and she put it down on the table.

She wondered if what she had overheard was really true or was it some strange twist of her imagination.

Then she recognised that the Duke was in danger, desperate danger.

If the Prince did not murder him one way, he would certainly do so in another.

At once she knew that at all costs she must prevent it happening.

She stood still for a moment trying to collect her thoughts and to think clearly.

Then she opened the communicating door and went into the Duke's bedroom.

Because he was tired he had undressed quickly and when his valet had left him he had climbed wearily into bed.

He was now nearly asleep.

Because he had drawn back his curtains and the moonlight was pouring into the room, suddenly he saw that someone was standing beside his bed.

"What is it?" he asked in a sleepy tone.

Then he realised who it was.

"Alnina!" he exclaimed. "Whatever is the matter? Why are you here?"

"Wake up, John, and listen," she began sternly.

He knew without her having to say any more that something was wrong.

He pulled himself up the bed, saying as he did so,

"What has upset you? Why are you not undressed?"

"Now listen," Alnina said, "listen to what I am telling you."

"I am listening – " the Duke replied.

Very quietly, because she was frightened of anyone overhearing and, picking her words carefully, she told him what she had heard.

The Prince was planning to kill him with the help, she thought, of the overseer to his estate.

"He did not sound a gentleman," she said, "and I am sure he will do exactly what the Prince has told him."

"Kill me because he wants to marry you?" the Duke questioned. "How can that be?"

"I have no idea, I promise you," Alnina replied. "He paid me compliments, but, as they were in French, I just took them for granted."

Her voice trembled as she went on,

"He never said anything more except that he was looking forward to tomorrow."

"So he will take you away while I die."

"What can we do? How can we escape?" Alnina asked.

"What we have to do first is to find William," the Duke whispered. "I know where he is sleeping. Go back to your own room as it is easier to talk there than here, which is connected with another room."

"Is anyone in it?" Alnina asked in a scared voice.

"Not that I know of, but we have to be careful. Now do as I say."

It was an order.

Alnina turned and walked back into her bedroom.

There were comfortable chairs in the bow window, but she just sat on the arm of one of them and waited.

Even now she could not help feeling that she was in a dream.

How could what she had overheard be real?

Yet she knew, because her Russian was so perfect, that she had not misunderstood a word of what had been said.

It seemed to her that a century passed before the Duke came back with William beside him. Both men were wearing frogged dressing gowns, giving them a somewhat military appearance.

The Duke walked up to Alnina and put his hand on her shoulder.

"There is no one near us," he said, "so tell William exactly what you overheard when you went downstairs."

In a trembling voice Alnina told her story again, repeating word for word what she had heard the Prince saying in Russian to the other man.

William and the Duke listened in silence.

When she had finished and ended by saying she had immediately hurried upstairs to tell the Duke, there was silence.

Then William exploded,

"This is the most monstrous plot I have ever heard. At the same time we knew when we came here that he was crazy to be united by marriage with Britain and who could achieve that more effectively than himself?"

"We have to escape," the Duke said, "And I now intend to send for Albert, my valet."

"Yes, we could not leave him behind," William said.

"As you well know, he is excellent with horses. If there is no one in the stables, which of course there should be, he will get them ready himself. We all four have to leave within the hour."

"Why an hour?" Alnina asked.

"Because I heard quite by chance that the sentries change at dawn and dawn comes early in this part of the world."

"Oh, I understand."

"Now you start changing into your riding clothes," the Duke said, "and I suggest that William and Albert go to the stables and saddle up four horses for us."

He stopped as if to think and then continued,

"The whole Palace will be sleeping at this time and if we have horses we will be well on our way to the yacht before they realise what has happened."

By the time he had finished speaking, William was on his feet.

"I will put on my clothes," he said, "and I suppose we should not take anything with us except what we stand up in."

"Nothing else matters," the Duke replied.

He went into his own room.

Alnina changed quickly into her riding clothes and she knew that whatever else she left behind, she must not leave the jewellery, as the Duke had emphasised that it belonged to his family.

She filled her pockets and then put the tiara and the necklace into a linen bag, which could easily be attached to the saddle of a horse.

Before she had finished the Duke came in and she saw he too was in riding clothes.

"I have looked downstairs," he said, "and there is no one in the hall. Albert has told me of a side door that we can slip out from and find our way to the stables."

"That sounds safe," Alnina murmured.

The Duke looked down at her.

"How could you possibly be so clever," he asked, "as to save me once again from disaster?"

"This time I have saved you, I think – from death," Alnina said. "I am frightened, terribly frightened, that we will not – get away."

"It is something we are going to do," the Duke said, "and no one will prevent us."

Instinctively he put his hand on his belt and Alnina knew that there was a revolver in it.

She only wished that she had one herself.

She was, in point of fact, quite a good shot, but this was not the moment to ask questions.

The Duke was already changing the key of the door to the outside and then waiting for her to join him.

She did so without speaking and he locked the door and put the key in his pocket.

Then he was leading her down the passage in the direction away from the hall.

At the end they found a secondary staircase leading down to the ground floor.

Although they thought that no one could hear them, they went on tiptoe, moving slowly until they reached the door leading into the garden.

As William and Albert had already gone out, it was unlocked and, when they were outside, they moved quickly behind the flowerbeds on the right side of the lawn.

The Duke put out his hand and took Alnina's.

Her hand was still trembling and his fingers seemed both strong and comforting.

They did not speak, but walked slowly and quietly behind the flowerbeds.

They reached a small path leading to the stables.

This was dangerous as whoever was on duty at this time of night would think it strange that they wanted to go riding and he would certainly make enquiries before they could leave with the horses.

Then to her relief they saw that two horses were already saddled and bridled and William and Albert were bringing two more out of the stables.

With them was a sleepy and unintelligent-looking stable boy who was obviously in charge at night.

As the Duke then lifted Alnina on to the side saddle of one horse, he said in a whisper:

"Thank the stable boy in Russian and give him this money."

He pressed it into her hand and she then bent down to where the boy was holding the bridle of her horse and gave it to him.

He looked at it with delight and she said in Russian,

"Thank you very much for your help."

The boy was obviously used to being given strange orders and thanked her.

Then he said,

"You'll have a nice ride up the mountains?"

"Yes, that is where we are going," Alnina agreed, "and we will see the sun rise over the tops of them."

The boy understood and smiled.

Then he stared at the gold coins he had been given and blurted out,

"Thank you. You very kind."

"If anyone asks why we have gone," Alnina said, "tell them we want to see the sun rise over your wonderful mountains."

She thought that the boy understood, but she said it twice more to make sure.

He was, however, so pleased with his gold coins that she was certain he could think if nothing else.

Now the three men were mounted.

Albert apparently knew the way better than anyone else. He led the way out of the stables to the back entrance of the Palace.

There were two rather tired sentries, who came to attention when they approached.

"Say that His Royal Highness wishes us to see the sun rise over the mountains," the Duke said to Alnina.

"That is exactly what I have been telling the boy."

"I heard you," the Duke said.

"And you understood?" Alnina questioned.

"You are a very good teacher!"

She smiled at him.

She was, however, still frightened that they might be stopped at the last moment.

However, the sentries accepted what she said and opened the gates.

They rode out, William and Albert leading the way.

They carefully avoided the main thoroughfare, but were all the time going, as Alnina knew, in the direction of Batum and the Black Sea.

They galloped along so fast that it was impossible to speak even though the Duke was beside her.

Later the moon faded and the stars went out one by one. Then the first light of the rising sun appeared behind them in the East.

Of course they were riding much faster and nonstop than they had in the Prince's carriage from Batum and it was not more than an hour or so later that they saw the Port just ahead of them.

'We have done it!' Alnina wanted to cry.

But it was just impossible to speak and difficult to breathe considering the pace they had been galloping.

At the same time because the Duke was saved, she wanted to cry out with joy, but she could only say a prayer in her heart.

'Thank you, God. Thank you.'

She had saved him.

Even as she thought about it, she then knew that she loved him.

CHAPTER SEVEN

There were only a few men and boys wandering about at the Port.

There was not a ship in sight except for the yacht which was at the far end of the quay near the open sea.

As they dismounted from their horses, Albert said,

"I'm sure, Your Grace, there'll be a stable of some sort for the horses here."

The Duke knew that there was one at every Port and he nodded.

"Then we must find it."

"I will ask one of these men," Alnina said, knowing that Albert was unable to speak Russian.

She gave her reins to William, who was nearest to her and walked across to one of the men.

She asked him in Russian where the stable was and he pointed to a building that was a little way from them and she thanked him.

The Duke, who had been watching, saw where the man pointed and was already moving in that direction.

Albert and William followed him leading Alnina's horse and she walked behind them.

She was thinking as she did so that she had saved the Duke first from marrying Princess Natasha.

Secondly from being killed on the mountain, but she would still lose him when they returned home.

Once they were on the yacht it would be the end of the drama, the excitement and the story, which from the very beginning she felt could not be real because it was so wonderful.

'I love him! I adore him!' she thought to herself. 'But he must never know it. At least I will have something to remember when I return home.'

At least there would still be the voyage when she would be near him and be able to talk to him as they had on the way out.

Now she wished that she had not wasted so much time teaching him and William Russian when she might have been talking to them or else been all alone with the Duke.

Even to think of it made her feel that strange thrill run through her body, as it had done yesterday and again just now.

It was something she had never felt before and she would never feel again once he had gone out of her life.

Of course he would be kind to her and might ask her occasionally to parties in London.

But it would never be the same as it had been when they travelled together, when he had taken her to see the monkeys at Gibraltar and they had talked of the Gods and Goddesses as they passed Greece.

But it was much more than that, more than listening to his deep voice, more than looking up into his eyes.

It was, she thought, in some strange way she could not explain even to herself, as if she belonged to him.

She had not realised it at first even though she had been excited at knowing him when he had called to see the wedding dress.

Every moment they had been together she had been more and more conscious of him so that he had filled her thoughts and her heart.

'I love him, but I must be very sensible about this,' she told herself as they reached the stable. 'He must never know what I am thinking and then be sorry for me. That is something I could not bear.'

There was a man in charge of the stable and there were two horses already stabled there and they were lucky that there were no more.

It was obvious that people who wanted to travel by sea would ride out from Tiflis and leave their horses, while they went to visit friends who lived further down the coast, or perhaps venture as far as Constantinople.

The man then took the horses into the stalls without asking them any questions.

The Duke gave him some money to look after them until they were collected.

"They belong," he said, "to His Royal Highness, Prince Vladimir, and you must take great care of them if he does not call for them immediately."

The man was instantly alert at the Prince's name and he promised to feed the horses and look after them well.

"I felt sure you would," the Duke managed to say in Russian.

Then they walked away from the stable and back towards the quay.

The Duke had thought that there was no need to alert the Captain of the yacht until he was rid of the horses.

Now he suggested,

"We will leave at once, even though they will not realise we have left until we don't come down for breakfast and they find our beds are empty."

134

Alnina gave a little laugh.

"That gives us at least an hour," she said, "before they even leave the Palace, so we need not hurry. Equally the sooner we are away the safer I will feel."

They reached the yacht and, as the gangway was down, they walked aboard.

The first to see them was one of the sailors who was scrubbing the deck.

He stared at the Duke and then saluted.

"Good morning, Your Grace."

"Good morning. Where is the Captain?"

"He be on the bridge, Your Grace," he replied.

The Duke was just about to walk towards it when William held up his hand,

"Wait just a minute, John, I want to talk to you and Alnina. Let's now go into the Saloon before you notify the Captain that we are on board."

The Duke looked at him in surprise, but did not say anything.

He merely walked towards the Saloon and he then opened the door and held it for Alnina to go in first.

It was as they had left it and she was rather touched to see that there were fresh flowers arranged on the table.

It was when they were in Gibraltar she had said that she loved flowers and the Duke had bought her a bouquet to take back on board and at every Port of call he had bought her more.

Although all those, by this time, were dead, the Captain or perhaps the Stewards had placed a large vase of fresh flowers in the centre of the table.

William, who came in last, closed the door behind him.

Now the Duke said,

"What is it, William? I want to leave here as you can imagine, so tell us quickly what is wrong."

"There is nothing particularly wrong," he answered, "but I have decided that I would like to stay here."

"Stay here!" the Duke exclaimed. "You cannot be serious."

"I am serious," William said, "because I have fallen in love with Natasha. I was going to tell you today that she loves me and we want your help in persuading the Prince I can marry her."

For a moment the Duke was silent and then he said,

"It is certainly a great surprise and something that I never expected. But of course, William, if you love her, you will have to persuade her father that you are of enough stature for him to accept you as his son-in-law."

"That is what I was going to talk to you about at breakfast and, by the way, before I ride back, I would like something to eat."

"You have taken my breath away and so I am not thinking clearly, but I will see to that if nothing else."

The Duke walked to the door, opened it and called for a Steward.

It was only a moment before one came running and looked at the Duke in surprise.

"We weren't expecting Your Grace," he said.

"I know that," the Duke answered, "but I am here and so are my two guests and we would like breakfast as quickly as possible."

"Yes, of course, Your Grace. I will tell the chef. I expect he's awake by now."

The Duke smiled.

"If he's not, then wake him up."

The Steward was already running to find the chef and the Duke went back into the Saloon.

"Now I think about it," he said, "I am both hungry and thirsty myself."

She shut the door and sat down opposite Alnina.

"The problem is," he said, "how to make William important enough to be accepted by the Prince."

He looked at his friend for a moment and then he asked,

"I suppose you are brave enough to live with a man who was prepared to kill me and I expect you as well, if necessary, by throwing us off the top of a mountain."

"Only because he wanted Alnina as his wife and I cannot believe that he treats many of his guests in the same way or we would have heard about it."

"I would not trust him further than I can see him," the Duke said. "But then, if you are brave enough to marry Natasha, you will have to make yourself so important that he does not dispose of you as he intended to do with me."

"I realise that, but I think if he has what he wants, an English son-in-law, he will behave reasonably."

William looked towards Alnina and said,

"After all, you could hardly blame him for wanting Alnina when she is so beautiful and, of course, he believes that, as an English Duchess, she will be almost as good as a distinguished son-in-law."

"I can understand," Alnina said, "that I was only the second choice. I want to say before we go any further that I think Princess Natasha is a charming and attractive girl and William will, I am sure, be very happy with her."

William smiled at her.

"Thank you so much, Alnina. I thought you would understand. As you have been clever enough to save the Duke, be clever now and tell me how I can make Prince Vladimir believe that I am of great stature in England."

"It's not going to be easy," the Duke remarked.

"I realise that," William said, "but Alnina has never failed us yet."

Alnina drew in her breath and then she asked,

"Surely there was someone in your family who was of consequence. A General or perhaps a Knight."

William stared at her.

"As a matter of fact," he said, "my grandfather was knighted when he became Lord Lieutenant of Oxfordshire. I was very young when he died, so I cannot say that he made a great impression on me."

"But you say he was knighted?"

"Yes, but, although he held that particular post, it was not, of course, inherited by my father."

"Nevertheless your grandfather was a Sir," and your great-grandfather was Lord Armstrong."

William nodded and Alnina went on,

"I cannot think that Prince Vladimir will be aware of the difference between a Knighthood and a Baronetcy. If you say that your grandfather was a Baronet, your father would in turn have been a Sir, and you, when he died, would have become Sir William Armstrong."

Then the Duke chipped in,

"William can say that he was not using his title when he was abroad because, as he was with me, one title in the party was quite enough for foreigners to remember!"

William looked at the Duke and asked,

"Do you think I could really get away with it?"

"Of course you can," the Duke replied, "and, when I go back to London, I will ask the Queen, if necessary on my knees, to grant you the title of Baronet."

"Even if she says 'no'," Alnina said, "no one out here would be able to find out if you were genuine or not. It would be too complicated."

"I am sure you are right," William said, "and I have never thought about it myself. But then, Alnina, you have always been our little angel from Heaven since you first advertised your mother's wedding dress."

Alnina laughed.

"It does sound rather ridiculous, but everything has happened because of that and the last disclosure has been very very frightening."

"That is something you need not fear any longer," the Duke said, "but to return to William, only you could be astute enough to make him sure of gaining the Prince's approval."

He rose as he spoke and went to the writing desk in the corner of the Saloon.

"I am going to give you a letter to take back to Prince Vladimir and in it I will mention who you are and tell him that you are an extremely respected and admired British subject when you are in your own country."

William laughed and was about to say something jokingly about it when the Stewards came in to lay the breakfast.

By the time they had laid three places and brought in the coffee, the Duke had finished his letter.

However, he could not read it while the Stewards were serving them with eggs and bacon.

Only when they had withdrawn did he suggest,

"Would you like to hear what I have written?"

"Yes, of course," Alnina said. "I was wondering how we could leave the Palace without there being any unpleasantness about it, because it might affect William."

"I thought about that too," he answered.

He held up the letter that was written on his crested writing paper and began,

"To His Royal Highness, Prince Vladimir Petrov.

Your Royal Highness,

It is with deep regret that we had to rush away from your delightful party without saying goodbye.

But a messenger arrived at midnight to inform me that I must, on the orders of Her Majesty Queen Victoria, return to England immediately.

Her Majesty requires me to welcome some Rulers from other countries who are arriving in ten days' time at Windsor Castle.

You will, I know, understand that I can do nothing but obey Her Majesty's command and I must arrive in England before or at least not later than Her Majesty's guests.

I just cannot thank you enough for the kind and generous manner you received me and my wife.

We will always remember how much we enjoyed staying in your beautiful Palace and being with Your Royal Highness.

My wife particularly wishes me to tell you that she will never forget how beautiful your flowers are in the garden and the delightful parties Your Royal Highness was gracious enough to give for us.

We are leaving behind us my dear friend, William Armstrong, who has, as Your Royal Highness will soon learn, fallen in love with the beautiful Princess Natasha.

I cannot imagine anyone else who would make you a more delightful or intelligent son-in-law.

A great number of our friends in England will be thrilled at the marriage.

He has asked me to apologise for the fact that he did not tell you that he is now, on his father's death, Sir William Armstrong.

He did not use his title because he thought that one title in the party was quite enough and in most foreign countries they find it difficult to appreciate the variety and distinction of our heritage.

The Armstrongs have been distinguished servants of Great Britain all down the ages. They have served in the Army and Navy and, of course, in the political world.

In the last two hundred years we have not had a King or Queen who has not been grateful to them in one way or another.

I can only hope that my dear friend, Sir William, will be able to assist you in your very beautiful country.

My wife has asked me to say that she will never forget the beauty you have shown her of the Caucasus Mountains.

Again a thousand thanks for our delightful visit and I hope Princess Natasha and Sir William will be as happy as my wife and I are at this moment.

We both send you our good wishes and grateful thanks.

Yours sincerely,

John Burlingford."

As the Duke finished reading, Alnina clapped her hands.

But William laughed.

"If he believes all that, he believes anything," he said. "Although there is, I would admit, a grain of truth in it. My great-grandfather was a General and my uncle was an Admiral."

"They have certainly served our country nobly," the Duke said. "If you had told me about your uncle being an Admiral, I would have that said that he was the right-hand man to Nelson at the Battle of Trafalgar."

"You are obviously an author of fiction and will have to write a novel, John, and, of course, nothing could be more dramatic or exciting than what we have endured in Georgia."

"What I really hope," Alnina said softly, "is that you will be very happy."

"I know I will be. Now if you will give me the letter I will ride back and you had better move off. So if the Prince is as much in love with Alnina as I am with Natasha, he might turn up at any moment!"

"Don't frighten us," Alnina replied. "But you are very sensible and the sooner we are out of the Black Sea the happier I will be."

"Very well" the Duke agreed, getting up from the table. "I will go and find the Captain and tell him to put to sea immediately."

He held out his hand to William.

"Take care of yourself, William, and let us know if it all goes as well as we hope."

"You know I will keep in touch with you, John, and thank you again for everything."

He kissed Alnina, then headed down the gangway, which was pulled in as soon as he was on the quay.

Alnina waved to him as he walked away towards the stable.

As she did so, she felt the engines turning below and the yacht began to move very slowly out of the Port.

She had the last glimpse of William as he reached the stable and then, as he waved and she waved back, the yacht was out to sea and moving more quickly.

It was then that she went to her cabin.

She was wondering as she did so what she had left to wear on the voyage, knowing that they had taken almost everything they possessed with them to the Palace.

She took off her riding clothes.

And then thinking that maybe Albert was right and she was in fact very tired, having had no sleep that night, she climbed into bed.

She had one last look out of the porthole before she did so and she realised that they were now a long way from the shore and Georgia was left behind.

She gave a deep sigh of relief.

Then, once she was in bed, she thought that nothing really mattered except that the Duke was now no longer in danger and that they were sailing back to England where he would be safe from the Prince.

'I love him! I adore him!' she whispered to herself as she fell asleep.

Because she had been very tired, for it had in fact been a ride in the dark that would have exhausted a man let alone a young woman, she slept all through the day until it was nearly time for dinner.

When she awoke with a start, it was to find that Albert had come into the cabin.

"What is it?" she asked sleepily.

Then she remembered where she was and sat up.

"I have been – asleep," she mumbled.

"You have indeed, Miss Alnina," Albert replied. "It be getting on for seven o'clock and His Grace, who's had a sleep too, be hoping you'll have dinner with him at seven-thirty. He's too hungry to wait till later."

Alnina laughed.

"It seems incredible that we slept so long," she said, "and, of course, I will be delighted to have dinner with His Grace. I think I have some dresses left here to wear."

"There be two or three I didn't pack, miss. I thinks they weren't quite grand enough for the Palace, but you'll look like a Queen in 'em as you always do."

"Thank you, Albert," Alnina smiled. "And now I would love a bath."

"That's just what I'm going to get for you, miss."

Albert went into the bathroom and Alnina lent back against the pillows.

Everything that had happened seemed to flash in front of her eyes, almost as if it was occurring on a stage.

And the most significant of all was that the Duke was safe on the yacht.

They were at sea and far far away from Prince Vladimir and his wicked plan and they were on their way back home, where everything would be as it was before.

As she was pondering, she remembered that there were still her brother's debts to be paid off and more things to be sold.

Then she told herself that she still had the Duke for at least ten days, however fast they steamed and it would undoubtedly be a glorious for her time to remember and savour.

The dress that Albert had left out for her was a very pretty one of blue chiffon embroidered with flowers, which made her look very young and, although she did not realise it, very lovely as well.

She took a great deal of time arranging her hair and because she felt that the dress needed it, she put on a small diamond necklace, but it was not one of the larger and more valuable jewels the Duke had brought with them.

As she then went into the Saloon, she felt a little shimmer of excitement because she was seeing the Duke again.

He was sitting on one side of a comfortable sofa reading a newspaper.

As he rose to his feet when she came in through the door, she saw that he had changed into evening clothes.

They were what he usually wore when they were at sea and Albert had not thought they were stylish enough to be taken to the Palace.

"Have you had a nice sleep?" the Duke asked.

He was smiling at her as she walked towards him and she replied,

"I slept and slept and I woke up so very thankful because you are safe."

"And you are safe too, Alnina. I don't think you would have been at all happy even though you would have become a Princess!"

"Don't let's talk about it," Alnina begged. "I have never been so frightened in my whole life as I was when I woke you up to tell you that the Prince intended to kill you."

"He also stated that there was no gold left in the mountain," the Duke answered. "I was therefore wasting my time and my energy in chasing what would turn out to be a 'wild goose chase'."

Alnina sat down beside him.

"But you loved your mountain," she said, "and I am sorry that you have lost it."

"I lost the unattainable," the Duke sighed. "Now there is no reason for me to think of it again."

He rose to his feet.

"I want you to come out on deck, Alnina, to see the sun set. It is much more beautiful than anything we have left behind us."

Alnina had been afraid that he would be bitterly disappointed at losing his mountain, but she smiled happily as he pulled her to her feet.

Putting his arm round her protectively, he took her out on deck, where they walked until they were looking out over the bow of the ship and they were then out of sight of anyone who might be on the deck.

The yacht was steaming straight across the middle of the Black Sea towards the Bosporus and the sun was setting in the West throwing a golden glow over the sky.

It was very lovely and the only sound was of the engines turning and the slap and swish of the waves.

"It's all beautiful, so beautiful," Alnina gasped.

She felt that the Duke was waiting to hear what she thought.

"What makes it so perfect," she carried on, "is that you are no longer in danger and you are safe, absolutely safe, because we are going back to England."

"Does it matter so much to you?" the Duke asked.

"Of course it does!"

"You saved me again," he said. "Now it would be impossible for me to be without you."

Alnina looked up at him.

She did not understand what he meant.

But, when she met his eyes, she felt once again that strange, exciting feeling which she knew was love.

"You are sorry, because I have lost my mountain, which had meant so much to me?"

"Yes, of course, I am, John."

"But I have found something else which matters so much more," the Duke said. "Something which makes me feel I was very stupid to want a mountain when there is something else so different and very much more desirable."

"What is – that," Alnina asked him.

It was difficult to say the words.

It flashed through her mind that, if he was seeking something different, he might not now want her or her help as he had needed it before.

"I suppose we all," the Duke said quietly, "follow our heart and it tells us what will make us happy."

He paused as if he was thinking it out and then continued,

"What the heart tells us in its own way is utterly and completely desirable."

"And you have found something like that?" Alnina asked, "even though you have lost your mountain."

"I have found something which is a thousand times more important to me than the mountain could ever be. I exaggerated the importance of it in my life because it was different from what other men were seeking – which, of course – is love of a woman."

There was silence.

Alnina felt as if a cold hand gripped her heart.

It told her that the Duke was looking elsewhere.

She had lost him for ever.

"What I am trying to say," the Duke went on very quietly, "is that, while I have lost the mountain, I have found something so wonderful that I cannot believe that I would ever be lucky enough to obtain it."

"And what – is it," Alnina managed to say.

The Duke smiled.

"Surely, my darling Alnina, you must have realised by this time that it is – *you*."

She looked up at him in sheer astonishment.

Then, as she saw the vivid expression in his eyes, she knew that was what she had wanted all along and what she had sought.

"I love you, Alnina," the Duke said slowly. "I love you and I know there is nothing else in my world of any consequence except you!"

"Is – that really – true?" Alnina whispered.

He did not answer, but merely drew her closer to him.

Then his lips were on hers.

As he kissed her, she knew that this was what she had longed for and prayed for.

But she had no idea that it could ever be hers.

The Duke kissed her and went on kissing her for a long time.

Then he raised his head.

He asked in a voice which sounded strange, even to himself.

"How can you do this to me? How can you make me feel as I have never felt before? It is, I know, the love that has always eluded me."

"I love you," Alnina whispered. "I have loved you for a long time, but I did not know at first it was love."

"I will teach you about love, my darling. Now I know that, while you can teach me many things, I too can teach you things that are so wonderful we cannot put them into words."

Then he was kissing her again.

Kissing her until she felt as if the whole world was turning round and round and they were alone on some enchanted mountain.

It was where there was no danger, only love and more love.

*

A long time later the Duke drew Alnina back into the Saloon.

Dinner was waiting for them.

And afterwards Alnina could never remember what she had eaten and drunk.

She had only known that her heart was singing.

She felt as if they were both flying in the sky, high above the earth and that nothing could touch them.

Only when the meal was over and the servants had withdrawn did the Duke say,

"Now, my precious, I am going to tell you what my plans are and then you must tell me if they will make you happy."

"As long as I am with you, John, I am so happy I feel it cannot be true," Alnina replied.

The Duke took her hand in his.

"Tomorrow," he said, "we are going to stop over at Constantinople and be married."

"*Married*," Alnina whispered.

"I have no intention of waiting until I return home. In fact I cannot wait any longer than tomorrow."

He paused for a moment before he went on,

"There is a little Church just outside Constantinople that I visited many years ago, because it was so old and had a long and fascinating history."

Alnina was listening intently.

"It is a Christian Church," he continued, "and we can be married there. Then, my precious, my darling, I can teach you all about love."

He pulled Alnina close to him and kissed her.

She knew that this was what she had hoped for and wanted, although she had been unable to put it into words.

*

They were married the next afternoon at one of the most attractive little Churches Alnina had ever seen.

When the Priest saw the Duke, he remembered him and greeted him with enthusiasm.

"I remember you well, Mr. Ford," he said, "and the nice gentleman you had with you when you came here five years ago."

"I am so glad that you remember me, Father," the Duke replied. "I have always thought when you blessed me before I left, that I would come back. And that is what I have done!"

The old Priest smiled at Alnina as he went on,

"I have come back with someone I want to marry and we are asking you if you would be kind enough to join us together for the rest of our lives."

The Priest beamed.

"That is what people always say when I marry them and you two will be blissfully happy together until you reach Heaven."

They then went into the small Church which, as the Duke had said, was very old. It had been restored to its original state only half a century ago.

They waited while the Priest changed into some very beautiful vestments and lit the candles on the altar.

Then, with only one young Server present besides themselves, they stood together in front of the altar.

The Priest read the Marriage Service with a deep sincerity which was very moving.

When the Duke and Alnina knelt to be blessed, she knew that his blessing would make sure that they never lost each other or their love.

*

Later that evening the yacht anchored in a quiet bay.

The Captain and all the crew drank the bride and groom's health and gave them their good wishes.

While they were on land, Albert had moved the Duke out of the Master cabin. It was where he had slept alone on their voyage out from England.

Now Alnina was in possession of it.

She was very touched to find that, before they had left the yacht to be married, the Duke had sent one of the Stewards ashore.

He was told to buy every flower that was available and they now decorated the cabin.

Alnina took off the pretty gown she had worn for dinner and then put on the nightgown that Albert had left out for her and slipped into bed.

The scent of all the flowers made the cabin more attractive than anywhere she had ever slept before.

She felt, in fact, as if she was a Fairy Queen in a Fairy world, where there was nothing dangerous or cruel there – only love.

Then, as the door opened and the Duke entered, she knew that this was part of their Fairy tale.

Nothing could be more wonderful or more ecstatic.

He walked towards her.

Then he stood looking down at her.

She thought there was a softness in his eyes that she had never seen before.

"Just how can I be so lucky," he asked, "as to have found you?"

"I have been asking myself the same question," Alnina replied. "I think it was Fate that we should come together, and Fate that it all started so incredibly with a wedding dress."

"And today you have been married without one, but now you are my wife, my darling, and I will never, never lose you."

He climbed into bed and took her into his arms.

For a while they were both silent.

It was almost as if the wonder and glory of it was impossible to put into words.

Then very gently the Duke began to kiss her.

First her forehead, then her small nose, her cheeks, and her lips were ready for his.

For a moment he just looked down at her before he sighed,

"You are perfect, perfect in every way and I love and worship you. I will never, my darling one, want for anything as long as I have you."

Then his lips were on hers.

He was kissing her, at first tenderly, then more demandingly, more passionately.

She felt as if the feeling, which had crept up in her heart before, was now part of them both.

It filled the room, the lovely flowers and the whole wonder and beauty of the world outside.

This was love.

The real love which comes from God and is a part of God.

Love has given them a special Heaven of their own which would be theirs for all Eternity and beyond.